*A Candlelight Ecstasy Romance*®

### "WHAT IS IT, AMY? THERE'S NOT ANOTHER MAN, IS THERE?" BYRNE ASKED.

"Why won't you marry me? I love the wilderness. You wouldn't have to give it up for a dull urban life. When I can afford a small plane, we can fly away on weekends. I know of pretty places even closer to Charlotte, state parks, lakes. . . . I'm dying to move out of my condo and build a house in the woods. What's the problem? Am I rushing you?"

"You don't even know me very well," she ventured. Her voice was soft and doubtful.

"If I don't, I sure am ready and willing to learn every detail about you."

Amy flinched at his words. He adored what he thought she was—a nature-loving rafting guide and switchboard operator who'd rescued his drowning niece. Would he still want her if he learned that she was the daughter of the notorious torch singer Evelina Sloan and had grown up in a nest of luxury outside Hollywood? She'd fought a long and bloody battle for her privacy. How could she marry a well-known radio talk-show personality who would pull her back into the glare of the limelight?

# CANDLELIGHT ECSTASY ROMANCES®

# HIDEAWAY

*Carol Norris*

*A CANDLELIGHT ECSTASY ROMANCE*®

Published by
Dell Publishing Co., Inc.
1 Dag Hammarskjold Plaza
New York, New York 10017

Dell ® TM 681510, Dell Publishing Co., Inc.

Candlelight Ecstasy Romance®, 1,203,540, is a registered
trademark of Dell Publishing Co., Inc., New York, New York.

ISBN: 0-440-13601-6

Printed in the United States of America
First printing—June 1985

*This book is for Doug,
who saved Dan's life in the Trinity River
yet wants neither credit nor reward.*

To Our Readers:

We have been delighted with your enthusiastic response to Candlelight Ecstasy Romances®, and we thank you for the interest you have shown in this exciting series.

In the upcoming months we will continue to present the distinctive sensuous love stories you have come to expect only from Ecstasy. We look forward to bringing you many more books from your favorite authors, and also the very finest work from new authors of contemporary romantic fiction.

As always, we are striving to present the unique, absorbing love stories that you enjoy most—books that are more than ordinary romance. Your suggestions and comments are always welcome. Please write to us at the address below.

Sincerely,

The Editors
Candlelight Romances
1 Dag Hammarskjold Plaza
New York, New York 10017

# CHAPTER ONE

When Amy Barrett recovered consciousness, she found herself snugly wrapped in someone's wool-lined coat. From the size of it, she was sure it was a man's coat that was swaddling her warmly. As awareness returned, she realized the man was inside his coat as well. With her. She lay clasped in his arms, pressed against his warm, bare chest.

Bundled from temples to thighs, she was locked in an embrace, listening to a man's heart pound. Her next discovery was that all her icy, sodden woolens were missing. She lay in some stranger's arms almost totally nude. The realization shocked her, but she had no strength to struggle.

The next shock was hearing an earnest growl. His breath warmed her ear; his lips touched it. He said, ". . . if we hadn't come, you'd be dead, you crazy, brave woman! *She* won't make it, but you tried. By God, you tried!"

Amy next realized she was shaking. When he loosened his grip on her, she shuddered like a dish of Jell-O. His grip instantly tightened. Hands chafed her back through the fuzzy coat. She drew up her knees so even her calves were covered by the skirt of the coat.

*She won't make it?* The man's words echoed in her hazy mind.

The drowning child! Suddenly Amy knew the reason she was so cold and wet. On her third attempt to talk she finally managed to whisper, "Isn't she okay?"

"I don't know." The man rocked her. "Thank God you're coming to. You risked your life. . . . Just take it easy, kid."

Her limbs refused to move, but she managed to force her memory into motion. How had she gotten into this man's arms? How long ago?

Only twenty or thirty minutes ago she'd been driving home from work after supper at Hamburgers Galore. This March evening she'd chosen a route less familiar but more scenic than her usual road. She'd been blithely smiling at the way long shadows striped the winding mountain road. The horizon shone golden beyond silvery pre-spring meadows and the blue mountain ridges of western North Carolina.

The trees around Hendersonville hadn't begun to leaf out, minting pale green coins against the background of dark evergreen boughs. In these mountains spring came late. This evening was clear and chilly, and a night wind stirred the leafy treetops.

Suddenly a little boy came leaping into the path of her car, a sudden pink blur of face and outstretched hands. She swerved her car to the right, so his momentum flung him not under her wheels but against her car door. After tramping on the brake and wrenching the door open, she fell sideways into the road and got both legs under her. The child was on his hands and knees beside the car, sobbing.

10

"I didn't see you, honey!" she exclaimed, fearing she'd hurt the boy.

"My sister!" he screamed, pointing behind him with a hand grimy from the road or her unwashed Chevy. "She's in the pond!"

For a moment Amy poised over the boy, who couldn't have been more than seven or eight years old, then pulled him to his feet. She took in what he was saying. Their collision was forgotten; his sister—what about his sister?

"Where is she?" Amy demanded.

"Mackay's Pond!" he screamed at her through his tears. "Pull her out of the water!"

Amy spun toward the narrow forest road he pointed to. "Show me!"

Shoving the boy into her car, she leaped behind the wheel, backed the car, and fiercely whipped the steering wheel to the left.

"Where? What pond?" she demanded.

"Down there!" he yelled, still weeping.

An eighth of a mile downhill she spotted the pond, its surface like a metal plate reflecting the last glow of twilight. Its borders were prettily landscaped with grass and shrubbery under hemlocks and maple trees. Beyond picnic tables and a barbecue pit, the shore sloped sharply down to meet the water.

"There!" He sprang out of the car as she drew into a parking place, and she jumped out of the seat to follow him.

"My little sister fell in!"

Amy saw, in a patch of mushy shoreline clay, fresh footprints, small and sneaker-soled. On the bank were

11

shiny streaks surely made by sliding feet. On the surface of the pond floated a long stick.

"I threw her a stick!" the boy cried. "Mom said don't jump in!"

"Good; that's right," Amy had muttered, staring at the unruffled surface of the water.

Nothing but the stick was visible.

"That's the stick. She's in there!" he said, sobbing and hopping frantically from one foot to the other.

"How long ago?"

The kid grabbed a handful of Amy's quilted blue coat and jerked her nearer the water.

"She fell in," the child insisted, "didn't come up!" He was barely coherent. "Save her, save her—my sister!"

"Run, get help," Amy cried, unbuttoning her coat. "Go on. Get! Stop a car. Tell the driver to call an ambulance quick."

The boy ran. He raced away, paused, looked back at her, his face contorted, and then disappeared. She could still hear his footsteps running on the gravel road as she shed her coat. It was cold, even without the wind chill from the evening breeze across the pond.

Free of her warm quilted coat, Amy slid down the bank and waded in. Her shoes filled with ice water. Her ankles submerging, she braced herself with a lecture: *You've been in cold water; that's your job. You know water safety. The colder, the better for the kid. What's the record? Forty minutes submerged?*

She didn't want to think about hypothermia. It could save the child, but it could kill her, the rescuer, whose wool sweater and slacks were a poor substitute for a rubber wet suit.

Gritting her teeth, she waded into the pond till she was knee-deep, her heart pounding a frantic warning: *Turn back! Turn back!* Openmouthed, she shrieked aloud at the incredible cold. It penetrated her slacks immediately and made them weigh ten pounds. Water so cold it felt as thick as gelatin stung her flesh. She wanted to leap back on shore.

Even as she stretched to reach for the floating stick, she knew she didn't dare submerge deeper than her waist. Pushing the stick underwater, she waded thigh-deep along the shore, with the stick stirring the water around her. With numbed feet she probed the water ahead.

Cans and bottles impeded her steps. There was no body.

No kid? Was there any drowned or drowning kid? Amy glanced at her watch: ten past six. How long had the kid been under? Five or ten minutes? Oxygen deprivation for four minutes normally meant brain damage, but in cold water, for a young child— She could hardly believe it herself, but there was a chance for survival.

Amy waded deeper. Numbness didn't end her pain. Each additional inch of her body immersed meant torture. Her legs barely worked anymore. Violently she shivered, rocked by tremors, her teeth chattering in her head. Her breath became harder and harder to catch, and hyperventilation surely wouldn't help. She was beginning to lurch as well as to shake. Common sense and coordination would be the next things to go.

Now her watch said 6:13. What chance did the kid have now? What kid?

Could the boy have lied to her? Impossible! He was wild with anxiety, and he'd picked the right person: She knew about drowning and was strong, twenty-nine, fairly tall, and a woman. Even a slim woman had much more fat on her than a man of comparable weight. Fat beat muscle as insulation.

She'd covered a large area of the pond. Surely the current that entwined itself about her knees wasn't strong enough to carry away a body. Poking her stick into the water made beautiful rings of ripples in the fading light. The child—did she even exist?

Amy's shins hit a submerged stump or a piece of drowned automobile, and she veered off. She stepped into a hole, sank shoulder-deep, then backed uphill. She couldn't breathe. Vigorous swimming would get her blood circulating, but her heavy clothes pulled her down, and she had to walk, not swim, to search. She lifted her chin and yelled for help, but her voice was a squeak.

The kid had been underwater for ten or fifteen minutes?

She herself was perishing. *Get out of the water, idiot,* she said to herself.

"Get outa there!" a voice echoed from shore.

The surrounding mountains weren't sheer enough to produce an echo. She slowly turned her head to stare at the people standing on dry land.

As in a silent film, the faraway figures gesticulated. She heard a woman screaming. A man seemed to restrain her, slipping and sliding on the bank with her. There were other men behind them.

14

"Ronnie!" the woman shrieked. "My baby!"

Amy's foggy vision took in two cars parked beside her Chevy. A man was starting to wade into the pond toward her.

"Come outa there! The pond'll be dragged. You'll freeze!"

The woman—the missing child's mother?—shrieked again.

Amy yelled, "We can save her! Where's the ambulance?" but she did begin to retrace her steps, trying to ignore the agony of the clinging cold. Her stick still beat the water, and her feet probed logs, rocks, and unidentified sunken objects. Again she stumbled and sank to her shoulders, biting her lip at the shock.

"Swim! Get outa there," one of the men yelled to her, "or we'll come get you." They were knee-deep now. She mustn't draw them in deeper and get them drowned.

"I can manage. Stay there!"

Something was suddenly blocking her left leg. It was soft, not prickly or hard. It sluggishly moved when she kicked at it. *Please, God,* she begged silently.

To get it, she'd have to submerge herself completely, go in over her head. Sucking both lungs full of air, Amy flung herself forward, eyes shut, arms reaching. Down, down, her head an ice cube, she reached blindly underwater with her fingers spread out.

Cloth. Clothing.

She yanked upward. It came along, slowly.

"Help me!"

Amy lurched toward shore, holding the child above water. One wading man caught hold of her arm and the child, to jerk them both toward shore. More men

15

leaped out of a car. Flashlight beams cut through the gray dusk.

"Do CPR!" Amy shouted. "She's got a chance. Make her breathe! Fast!" Her legs folded; people propped her up.

"Too late," said one voice.

But the woman screamed, *"Do* it! *Do* it! Please, God, save her!"

"Let's humor 'em," muttered a man. The limp little figure was illuminated, showing a white face, red coat, and green trousers going upside down over a man's arm. Water dribbled out of the small nose and mouth.

". . . anyone do CPR?" Amy begged. "Cardiopulmonary resus—" She sagged, unable to continue.

"Sure. Army training," said one man.

Icy from the crown of her head to the hems of her sodden slacks in the rising wind, Amy now lost the ability to speak. The ground tilted dangerously. She could barely say, "Hypothermia—"

Before she fell, her water-logged sweater dragging her shoulders down, a body blocked her view, elbowing others aside. He seized the bottom of her sweater and yanked upward. Through the blur of her wet eyelashes, all she could see was heavy black brows in a face tense with determination.

"Get her out of this." Illustrating what "this" was, he started to strip off the heavy sweater. The upward tug kept her on her feet as he struggled to remove it over her torso and over her head.

When she could see again, the man's sheepskin coat was open, and he pulled her against him and closed his body-warmed garment around her, enveloping them both. He sank down, holding her so she lay diagonally

16

across him, on his thighs, bundled to her ears. He loosened his grip only to reach between her body and his to yank up his sweater.

Her breasts came to rest against his warm flesh. She gasped for breath through skull-rattling, chattering teeth that played an accompaniment to his heartbeat. He hugged her tightly—this big, warm-bodied stranger—kissing her temple, rocking her. She could see nothing and heard no words but his.

"You tried! Let's get you warm now. She's gone, but by God, we won't let you die, too!"

"She's not gone!" Her lips moved inaudibly against rough wool. ". . . still can revive her!"

While she wasn't looking, her frigid slacks must have been removed. Her frozen legs folded themselves snugly under his coat. The man continued to rock her, groans rumbling in his chest, like a mourner—or a lover.

Shock overcame her. Mercifully Amy dozed off into the arms of darkness. As she floated between painless drowsiness and the pain of thawing, nestled in her rescuer's coat, drawing on his bodily warmth, her thoughts kept returning to the victim, the little girl. Where was she? Amy moved her lips, trying to speak, while his warm breath brushed her temple.

"Who are you, honey? God, what you tried to do!"

Amy couldn't make herself heard, couldn't move, with both arms pinned by her sides. The man was both big and strong, and his arms encircled her shoulders and hips.

Amy could hear a woman sobbing. There had to be a dozen people milling around, voices muffled. How much time had passed? Five minutes or twenty? Was

17

the child dead? Had they lost hope and stopped trying to get a heartbeat?

Suddenly the man holding her inside his coat jerked into motion. "Hey, listen to that," he shouted in Amy's ear. All his muscles contracted. He leaped to his feet, taking her with him—lifted suddenly vertical, as if she were dancing with him, very close.

Before she could see anything, she heard a shout.

A man was shouting, "We've got a heartbeat! Her heart's beating now!"

"Let me see!" she gasped, fighting to get free. He let go of her. The sudden chill told Amy she was indeed nude except for bikini briefs. No one, however, was staring at her; the child lying wrapped in coats on the ground drew every eye. A woman striped with flash-light beams tried to throw herself upon the little girl, and a man pulled her back.

"Unwrap her!" Amy yelled. "Keep her cold. Do it! Don't warm her up now. It'll kill her."

Amazingly the men obeyed. They stripped back the coats from over the soaking wet child. Flashes inter-mittently lit the twilight scene: glare, dusk, glare, dusk, glare.

Amy had let out a whoop of joy. A photographer whirled, lifted the camera, and illuminated her with his flash.

Covering her breasts, calling him an impolite name, she ducked behind someone, then bumped into a car, her own car. Gratefully she slid through the still-open door. On the back seat was a lap robe she pulled over herself. She shut the car door and turned the key that hung in the ignition.

She felt no pain and had no plan; she slowly turned

the wheel, missing people by inches. She passed the arriving ambulance as she ascended the road away from the pond.

Feet bare on the pedals and lap robe tucked around her neck like a giant bib, Amy gritted her teeth as she accelerated. Shivering violently, she clung to the steering wheel, one moment wondering whether she could get home, the next moment losing track of what had happened. She remembered that hypothermia caused memory lapses and unconcern about discomfort before she lapsed into unconcern.

"I saved her," she whispered. No, something mysterious called the mammalian diving reflex had saved her when the child's face went underwater. A wonder that she herself hadn't gone into a life-sustaining coma after she had ducked beneath the surface, but who would've saved her? If no one had come, both she and the child would surely have perished.

She reached the county road and remembered to put her car heater and fan on maximum. She turned left. Trembling, giddy, and aware of the danger of going back into shock, Amy aimed her car toward home.

## CHAPTER TWO

Amy's renovated eighty-year-old log cabin, a silhou-
ette of vine-covered logs under a moonlit tin roof, was
surely a wonderful sight. She managed to get out of
the car and stagger up the path to the door, as Cornflake, her yellow cat, and Abercrombie, the color-co-
ordinated golden collie, wound themselves around her
legs, then forced their way into the house, eager for
love and supper.

"Me first!" Amy cried, bare feet treading the soft
green carpet past blocky pine furniture, dried flower
arrangements, and original oil paintings. She went
straight to the bathtub.

She ran water at full pressure, both hot and cold.
Yearning for a steaming hot bath, she knew the water
must be no hotter than normal body temperature.
Otherwise, she'd warm up too fast. Gentle defrosting
was necessary.

Alcohol was another no-no—a depressant. Not taking time to put the kettle on, she drank two glasses of
hot tap water, as much as she could hold, to serve as
antifreeze.

The collie pushed his fluffy side against her bare legs
as she reached into the bedroom to switch on her electric blanket. Be prepared. At any minute she might

keel over. Her coordination was rotten. At least she had no buttons or zippers to contend with.

To stave off shock, Amy sat down beside the filling tub and put her head between her knees. Abercrombie, positioned on the bath mat right in front of her, whined, very much concerned about his dog food.

Ignoring him, she dropped off her two remaining garments, the lap robe and the blue nylon bikinis. Her skin felt as cold as the tall porcelain tub with its lion-claw legs; she looked almost as white, too. Well, better white than blue. She lurched into the tub and submerged with a groan of relief. Now maybe her shivering would ease off.

When she got her wits back again, she began to wonder if the story would be on the TV news tonight. She'd want to learn about the child's condition. Rushed by ambulance to a hospital, plied with drugs, put on a respirator, she might make it, her brain might not "gork out," as her doctor friend would put it.

Was she a lifesaver, or was she dreaming? Amy didn't need to pinch her arm to prove she was awake; the pin-prickling sensations all over her body indicated she was alive, awake, and thawing.

How about that man who'd held her? She decided to postpone thoughts about him. No, think about who the child was, poor little tyke . . . and poor mama and the frantic pint-size brother.

Abercrombie, the collie, hung his long head over the rim of the tub, his narrow eyes contemplating her, inspiring guilt in the neglectful. Cornflake paced resentfully along the tub's rim, vertical tail twitching. With her toes Amy turned the hot-water faucet on

21

again. More heat was needed to thaw herself like a frozen fish fillet for dinner.

Who was the man who'd rescued her, stripped her and cradled her in his arms, inside his coat, doing exactly the right thing, while other men resuscitated the three- or four-year-old kid? Was he the father or just some man who'd happened by? He'd been big, black-browed, and warm; that's all she remembered. He'd said kind things to her, his lips brushing her ear. Trying to hug her warm, he'd massaged her back, sharing his body heat. She might recognize him on television.

. . . and see herself on TV as well? Naked?

Amy extracted the drain plug with her toes, tugged down a towel, and dried herself while reclining. Then she made it to her bed, but not before dumping out some dog food and cat food right on the floor. Cornflake didn't mind but the collie hesitated to eat off the kitchen linoleum.

This had been a farm cabin before the turn of the century, but the fields had reverted to forest. She'd bought it cheap, and its location on the river meant she and her partner could run their summer river-rafting business right from Amy's veranda.

The prickling all over her body wasn't comfortable, but it was a good sign. "Go make me some hot coffee," she told Abercrombie when he reported back to bedside, but not surprisingly he declined to do so.

Too bad she lived alone. A good thing she wasn't living with Rodney. Six years ago her wedding gown had been purchased, wedding invitations sent out, and gifts coming in when he finally unleashed his temper.

Gorgeous, tall Rodney Nielson, fresh out of the

army, had hauled off and hit his fiancée—but, as he said, only with his open hand and only twice. She knew, however, that after marriage he'd feel free to make a fist. She wasn't about to become a battered wife, so she'd called off the wedding. Word about the reason got around, and Rodney left town. So did Amy —heading in the opposite direction.

By age eighteen she'd already fled the glitter and glitz surrounding her famous or rather infamous mother, who lived in Malibu. At twenty-three she'd left her fiancé and traveled the rest of the way across the country, not settling down till she reached the North Carolina mountains. She found herself not one job but two. During the school year she ran the switchboard at a local college; each summer she took to the river.

Tonight a little girl was alive because Amy Barrett was foolish enough on March 11 to go wading with her clothes on.

Someone still had those clothes—one coat, one sweater, one pair of slacks, and her shoes and socks. Was it the man who'd murmured tender words into her ear?

Bundled up in bed under the electric blanket, she took an unplanned one-hour nap, then awoke with a start and thumbed the remote-control tuner. It was time for the evening news on television.

A reporter had told her that by tuning to the police frequency he often could beat the ambulance and police to the scene of an emergency. Tonight one photographer had beaten the ambulance to the lake, so there were bound to be pictures.

"Tonight a miracle occurred" were the first words

23

of TV anchorwoman Diana Hall. Her pretty face was earnestly solemn. Her voice continued, as the screen showed a dim view of Mackay's Pond. The TV film crew had been quick.

Amy sat erect, drawing up the hot electric blanket. On the screen she glimpsed the back of a sheepskin coat. The man seated on the ground looked distinctly pregnant. What was that bulge across his middle? Was it *she* herself? Amy stared incredulously.

The video camera focused on the desperate mother, identified as Sheila Cooper of Orchard Lane, as she climbed into the back of the ambulance. Everyone was gesticulating. The commentator exulted, "Little Rhonda Sue Cooper, age four, is given a good chance for survival."

Again the newswoman appeared on the screen. "At this hour," she said, "we take you live to Fletcher Medical Center, where Art Mulder has a live report."

Art Mulder, mike in hand, informed viewers that "tiny Rhonda Sue is now being treated for hypothermia—extreme chilling. She is thought to have been completely submerged for fifteen minutes or longer. Fifteen minutes! Her survival is a medical miracle. As her family awaits word of her condition, they seek the young woman who rescued her."

The reporter paused. Amy recognized the floodlit hospital portico behind him. "The child was located in the icy pond at about six thirty this evening by a mysterious woman who has since disappeared. She herself was suffering from extreme exposure. Anyone knowing her identity should get her to a hospital! This unknown woman is the hero of the hour, folks. She's dark-haired, of medium height, in her twenties, and is

24

thought to be driving a blue Ford." The reporter gazed straight at Amy, making her cheeks heat up.

"This is Art Mulder at Fletcher Medical Center," he excitedly concluded, "the scene of a miracle wrapped in a mystery."

The next story involved an auto accident at Four Seasons Shopping Center. Amy switched channels.

Channel 9 News lacked film of Mackay's Pond, but it featured an interview with a harried-looking physician. He was maintaining the child's body at a low temperature and sedating her to allow her brain to recover from its trauma.

Amy snuggled down under the warm blanket, wondering if her own temperature was now normal. She was dark-haired, of medium height, and drove a blue Ford, huh? Then no one would ever connect her with the miracle worker. Her blond hair darkened when wet. Compared to that big man who held her, she'd seem only of medium height at five-seven. Her Chevy was green.

A good thing this was Friday night. She didn't work till Monday, so she'd have time to recuperate, staying in bed watching for reports on the child's progress. If the Coopers learned her identity, they'd turn themselves wrong side out to thank her when anyone— anyone who knew about cold water—would've done what she'd done.

Punching the channel changer, she heard the same facts all over again, the same report, but this time she learned the name of her rescuer. He was also a Cooper —none other than Byrne Cooper, the popular radio talk show host from Charlotte! Amy groaned. That's the sort of person she wanted at all costs to avoid—

25

someone in the media—a public personality. The press had pursued and photographed her mother and her from the day of her birth. If her birth hadn't made the newspapers, it had certainly been reported in the tabloids and the pulp magazines. Her mother kept all the clippings.

"I hardly saw the woman," Byrne Cooper told the reporter. "Yes, I held her, but somehow she managed to slip away. She was there one second, gone the next." He gestured with a long arm.

Amy saw his face clearly for the first time, and she actually blushed. Taller than the reporter, Byrne Cooper was still wearing that sheepskin coat—leather outside, wool inside. Amy's skin tingled in remembrance of that warm, furry coat closing over her bare back and his bare chest pressing against her breasts, all warm muscle under a pounding heart.

Byrne Cooper's face was a construction of black brows and a square jaw under dark hair. His nose was solid, in profile slightly but dramatically hooked. He showed his lower teeth when he emphasized a word. Looking into the camera—into her bedroom—he demanded to know who she was. "If you're listening, ma'am," he said, "please call us. Call any Cooper in the phone book. We owe you so much."

"Okay, even-steven," Amy said with a grin. He owed her gratitude because he was a Cooper, not young Ronnie's daddy but kinfolk. For her survival Amy owed him gratitude. One good deed would balance the other.

Fine. She could remain a mystery woman, someone

26

far more intriguing than Ms. Barrett, the switchboard operator, or Amy, the tomboy on her rubber raft, yelling herself hoarse at a half dozen half-scared rafters, "Paddle, harder! Now! Paddle!"

# CHAPTER THREE

Byrne Cooper figured he'd better hang the Norwegian wool sweater and the slacks, as well as the running shoes and the socks, outdoors in the sun this morning to dry. All these had come off the young woman when they'd stripped her last evening, trying to raise her temperature.

Who was the young woman he'd held to his heart, clasped, cold and trembling, in his arms? Byrne hunted through his memory for a few shreds of evidence by which to identify her. Her face had been covered by steaming wet hair.

"Hair how long?" Sheila and Mike had asked. Then: "What color hair?"

"Dark hair," he'd said, and repeated that supposition to the press.

"How tall?"

"How old?"

"Didn't you get a photograph of her?" he demanded, only to receive evasive answers. There was apparently only one photo, a shot which was useless for identification purposes.

Whoever the girl was that he'd stuck quickly inside his coat to revive, she'd been strong yet slim, slender-waisted and marble-white in the flashlight beams.

He'd flattened her firm breasts against his chest. She'd jarred his whole body with her shivering. Her wet cheek against his had been so cold that he'd feared for her life. Who knows how long she'd been wading in the pond, searching for Ronnie Sue?

Little Billy wasn't sure of the make and color of her car. Stupidly no one who rushed to the rescue had glanced at the car, which was already there.

Why had the young woman fled?

He remembered a story he'd read as a kid at summer camp about an escaped criminal who saved a man's life and then had to disappear to avoid recapture. Surely someone so unbelievably gallant was completely legit. Was she so confused by her own hypothermia that she hadn't known what she was doing?

He'd chased after her, thinking she'd run into the woods, but when the ambulance took Ronnie to the hospital and the rest of them headed back to their cars, they realized that the first car there was now gone. Vanished.

Byrne leaned back wearily in his brother Mike's recliner chair, keeping watch downstairs while Mike caught a few hours' sleep.

Hanging around the hospital all night had left Byrne weary but unwilling to go to bed and maybe not catch the telephone before it woke up Mike. Sheila had a cot at the hospital beside Ronnie's bed, and Mike would head for the hospital soon. It was already dawn.

At least Ronnie Sue was too young at four to realize what danger she'd been in, and Sheila, six months pregnant, hadn't lost her unborn baby. He writhed in his chair, remembering that he'd joined in when the guys ordered Ronnie's rescuer to come out of the water empty-handed.

"Quit hunting for a dead body and save yourself!" they'd stormed at her, and the guys who'd arrived first were starting to wade in to get her. They'd said the water couldn't have been more than fifty degrees.

When the woman had vanished underwater, he'd figured she was a goner—until up she'd come, with Ronnie Sue! He shook his head at the picture of woman and child, rising out of the depths.

Did she have kids? Surely only a mother would risk her life for a child she didn't even know.

Byrne stuck a pillow behind his head and crossed his arms over his chest. Sleep! He had to take a nap so he could accomplish something this Saturday morning. He had to find that lovely young woman. How can you repay an act like hers? Not with any monetary reward! How on earth do you thank someone for saving the life of your precious little niece?

Amy's intention to stay in bed all day didn't last past ten in the morning. Abercrombie had to go out, and he couldn't squeeze through Cornflake's cat door. She staggered out of bed, opened the door for the collie, and put the teakettle on. It was a dazzlingly sunny day, warmer than yesterday—ideal weekend weather. Everyone would head for the Blue Ridge Parkway or Chimney Rock or take a picnic to Mackay's Pond. . . .

Only kiddie shows, no news, were on TV. Amy's thirst for word about Ronnie Sue Cooper grew more acute. The little girl might've died. Not till 6:00 P.M.

30

would she get any local news except on the radio. She'd have to go out for a paper.

First she took another bath, a hot, soapy one this time to make sure she was warmed up. No signs of frostbite marred her fingers or toes. Bone-deep weariness was her only leftover from the previous evening's adventure. She put in a TV dinner to bake, wished she could afford a microwave oven, and started to make her bed. When the timer went off, she found she'd been sleeping again, draped on top of the covers.

Okay. She'd eat, then dress in her red sweater, plaid vest, black jeans, and boots. She'd brush her hair into a shoulder-length golden mane and put on lipstick and mascara.

It was three in the afternoon before she got all this accomplished.

She carried the newspaper out of the store before opening it, carried it wrapped around the carton of cottage cheese and the package of sweet rolls she'd bought to give her some energy. She cut through the woods back to her place, following the pretty path through saplings still bare in the late-afternoon sunshine. Choosing a rock to sit on, Amy pulled out a sweet roll, stuck it in her mouth, and unfolded the paper.

There she was, on page one.

Almost naked.

Mercifully, however, only her back showed, and that was half-hidden behind another figure. A white curve of side and hip was bisected by the smallest of bikinis. The caption read: "Child Lives; Rescuer Sought."

"Well, they can seek and seek and not find me from this picture," Amy remarked, beginning to grin.

Most important, little Ronnie Sue had not lost ground.

"Oh, thank heaven!" Amy groaned, tears welling up in her eyes.

The round-faced, light-haired cherub appeared on page one of the morning paper with her mother, father, and brother. It was a studio portrait. Yesterday Sheila Cooper—six months pregnant, God help her!— had shrieked for the resuscitation of Ronnie. After all that, the poor woman was probably a wreck today.

"We want to know who saved our little girl," the father was quoted as saying.

Brother Billy explained that he'd taken his sister with him to see if the ducks had come back to the pond.

"But Billy ran and got help," Amy mused, hoping he got credit for that.

So, Byrne Cooper of "Conversations with Cooper" fame was the paternal uncle of Ronnie Sue. . . .

Amy walked back home, her boot soles sinking into soft, dark, decomposing leaves left over from autumn. In front of her cabin she exercised Abercrombie the way he adored. She shoved him into a clockwise spin, then repeated it till he was dizzy—and hoarse from yipping. Cornflake watched from the edge of the tin roof.

Her window boxes would have to be reseeded, and the well cover checked. There was rot in the cabin's foundation. That was the price of country living.

She wouldn't, however, trade this for any apartment in town; no way, even though Abercrombie wasn't much of a watchdog. Hendersonville was small, safe, and mellow, a lovely place for children and old folks.

Amy went to bed early, after learning from TV that the Cooper family was trying to trace her by the labels in her clothes. Fat chance! Her sweater was a gift from a Norwegian friend and said "Geilo, Norway." The coat she'd bought years ago on a trip to New York. The slacks were from the local thrift shop.

Funny. She felt like a criminal in hiding, watching the police and detectives search. Would policemen help look for her? A good thing that she had no guilty conscience and that no punishment awaited her.

She wondered about Byrne Cooper, who looked so formidable on TV. Was he really as decent a human being as he seemed on the radio?

At noon the next day, Sunday, she again left her hideout, driving to a shopping center for milk, paper towels, hot dogs, and raisins.

At the supermarket she'd reached the check-out counter before she saw it.

Gaping, she didn't take in what she was seeing until a little old lady ahead of her in line commented.

"Isn't that just plain disgusting?" said the woman. "What'll folks think of Hendersonville?"

A tabloid—call it a scandal sheet or gossip rag—made Amy blink in disbelief. She dropped her chin so her hair would swing forward and hide her flaming cheeks.

There, in stark black and white, shone a full frontal shot that almost covered the whole front page under the screaming headline MYSTERY WOMAN!

Strands of hair covered the woman's face. Amy remembered flinging up an arm defensively over her face, leaving the rest of her uncovered when the flash-bulb had exploded.

Amy stared at her bare breasts, slim waistline, faintly visible bikini panties, and her long legs. Were this anyone else, she might have nodded yes, the woman did have a nice figure, well proportioned, looking not older than what? Twenty-five?

"They shouldn't allow a photograph of a naked woman to appear on newsstands," the old woman told the clerk, who frowned, appearing to agree.

"Think of the effect on little children," the woman added grumpily. "Pure filth!"

Amy ached to grab the paper and read what it promised to reveal inside. "See page 7," the caption read.

The local paper's photo of her was nothing compared to *this*, yet the same photographer had probably taken both shots. Amy was doubly amazed—first, that such a picture had been sold to this national weekly, and secondly, that she wasn't more upset. Anonymity made the difference. Cutesy shots of Amy Barrett next to her torch-singing mother, Evelina Sloan, had bothered Amy more than this nearly nude photo did—only because this one bore no name. It was almost fun to play mystery woman.

Besides, this woman looked brunette, and Amy was blond. Her face didn't show.

Holding her packages in front of her bosom, she reached out and whisked a copy of the weekly off the rack. She put on a grin to remark chirpily, "I'll just have to see what this says about Hendersonville. We don't often make the national news, do we?"

The old lady scowled and sniffed as she departed.

"It's about that child drowning," the woman behind the check-out counter said. "I sneaked into the back room to read it. I can't imagine how they got the story in print so fast. It happened just a day or two ago. And where'd they get the picture? Our papers don't print anything like that."

Amy stuck the tabloid into her grocery bag and drove all the way home before unrolling it to read about herself and Ronnie Sue Cooper.

There was darned little about Ronnie Sue, the "MIR-ACLE BABY" who "SURVIVED FIFTEEN MINUTES UN-DERWATER." There was a picture of the distraught mother and a good shot of black-browed Byrne Cooper, earnestly gesturing toward the pond. And then there was the naked marvel.

Amy smiled incredulously at her nationwide fame. The photo was flattering, she had to admit, and she received more credit for the rescue than she deserved.

Then she read the long quotation attributed to Byrne Cooper, local radio personality: "I didn't really see her face. I'd know her best by her lovely breasts that I warmed by holding her against me. What I re-member is that she had the most perfect body I've ever seen. To save her, I immediately had to strip her na-ked. I opened my clothes so I could warm her body against my bare flesh. If I hadn't been so worried about my little niece, I could have fallen in love on the spot. What a gorgeous mermaid came out of that water, carrying my brother's child in her arms! I wish I could hold and kiss her again, the way I held her and kissed life back into her on Friday night. If anyone knows her identity, please notify me. She'll get a reward that I guarantee would thrill—and fulfill—any woman."

"Oh, brother! Oh, that's incredible! What a—a barrel of . . . trash!" Amy cried, flinging the newspaper aside. Then she picked it up again, reread the man's words, and started to ball it in her fists. Immediately she flattened it out again. Unbelievable!

What gall! What a louse! Now she knew that Byrne Cooper's kind, concerned radio persona was a lie.

She went to the telephone, flipped open the phone book to the Coopers' number and dialed.

"Hello?" the baritone voice said after only two rings. She knew the voice immediately. She'd listened to it for years on the radio.

"That is certainly a great way to thank somebody!" Amy said more loudly than she'd ever before spoken on the phone.

She didn't give him a chance to respond.

"Mermaid, huh? Reward, huh? Well, I can tell you what to do with your reward, ol' buddy! You can stick it—"

"Who are you? Is this— Are you the woman who—"

"The woman whose photo is spread across the front page of the sleaziest tabloid. Boy, you really know how to thank a person, don't you, Mr. Cooper!"

"That scandal sheet? The one out today? Look, I didn't talk to that reporter!" the man said urgently. "He badgered us all morning at the hospital. Look, believe me! Those aren't my words, honey."

"Honey, yourself!" she cried, doubly angry because she wanted to believe him. "I'm certainly glad I didn't stick around."

"Who are you? Where are you? In town? Please. Please, give me your name. We're all frantic to thank you, to meet you. Don't believe the garbage that scandal sheet prints!"

She didn't dare continue to listen. Her stomach was getting upset. Vengefully, without another word, she hung up on him. Certainly she wouldn't tell the man her name.

"Well, that's that," she said. "I'm minus a few items of clothing, including a coat and sweater I'm going to miss, but I am never going to reveal my identity to *that* guy. No way. The big-shot blabbermouth lecher!"

She invited her cat to sit on her shoulder and patted the collie; she was blinking back tears.

From the rug halfway across the room from her, a tall, naked woman stared at her, one eye peering out through strands of wet hair. Amy Barrett, who'd fled the publicity that had marred her youth, was now nationally famous.

# CHAPTER FOUR

Byrne drove his brother to the hospital to join Sheila in their vigil at Ronnie's bedside. Sitting by her, talking to Ronnie, they'd wait out her coma. His little niece had to be kept cold and sedated while damaged brain tissue healed. Her mattress was filled with ice water. Today the pupils of her eyes were no longer fixed and dilated like those of a baby doll, and she was no longer rigid, blue, and unable to breathe for herself. However, on the advice of medical experts down in Atlanta, she was being held in a state of suspended animation. Instead of transferring her to Atlanta, far from her family, the doctors could consult by telephone.

What freaked out Sheila and Mike and Byrne was that Ronnie would remain for a week in a barbiturate-induced coma, her temperature at 85 degrees, far below the normal 98.6.

Byrne tried to remain objective enough to be useful as the family chauffeur, sitter, and gofer and to deal with the press. His experience in radio journalism hadn't helped him deal with that tabloid's reporter, however. What an expletive-deleted bunch of lies *he'd* written!

So far all the Coopers were hanging in there.

Brother Mike hadn't fallen apart yet, though he looked like death. Sheila, carrying the new baby, was certainly treading on thin ice emotionally. Today all four grandparents plus Sheila's brothers would be arriving. If only they didn't also have to worry about the condition and whereabouts of the woman who'd rescued Ronnie.

Byrne, who'd held the mystery woman in his arms and then let her escape, felt nearly as much guilt as Sheila and Mike did for letting their children wander off to Mackay's Pond. To try to be useful, he carried a small notebook in his jacket pocket to take notes on everything the physicians said. This data ought to be widely disseminated. Lives could be saved if more people did what that missing young woman had done.

"When a mammal's face goes under fifty-degree water, the body may go on hold," a doctor told them. "Metabolism slows. Hypothermia then can take over, lessening the brain's need for oxygen."

Byrne scribbled notes each time the doctors gathered the family together for updates on Ronnie's condition. "Trust us," the doctors begged. "We're learning what to do in cases like this."

Byrne wished he had his tape recorder along. He'd have to do a radio show on this topic. The opening would describe two forms of emergency treatment that had totally changed: care of burns and manner of resuscitation.

Everyone used to apply grease or butter to a burn. Now doctors realized ice water was best for burns. People used to compress the ribs from behind, trying to resuscitate a person. Now one blew directly into the lungs, with much better success.

Byrne asked himself, "How many kids pulled out of cold water die because well-meaning people rush to warm them up while they're being resuscitated—*if* resuscitation is attempted?"

Hell, they'd done that on Friday night—thrown coats over Ronnie Sue's body. What was harmful for Ronnie was good for Ronnie's rescuer, the mysterious young woman he'd held in his arms. Her situation had been the opposite of Ronnie's. Hypothermia and the mammalian diving reflex had saved Ronnie's life; hypothermia could have killed the woman. He'd acted correctly by stripping the woman and pressing her, skin to skin, against his chest. She was still breathing, but Ronnie had been fast-frozen; her heartbeat and breathing had ceased.

He felt an obligation to publicize these facts—facts totally absent from the blasted tabloid story that was being read from coast to coast today.

Ronnie was in good hands. She could come back to them undamaged or at least repairable. As for the nameless woman rescuer, she apparently hated him when all he'd wanted—all that any of them wanted—was to swamp her with love and gratitude. He hadn't mentioned to anyone her angry phone call; it was too embarrassing. First he had to find her and convince her of the truth. The key to that goal was his nephew, seven-year-old Billy.

Byrne left Mike and Sheila hovering over Ronnie at the hospital and drove himself back to Orchard Lane, where both families had gathered. Billy wouldn't lack for baby-sitters. From the treelined street of brick houses hiding behind tree branches green with new leaves, he pulled into the driveway. A plastic-wrapped bundle sat on the doormat. He picked it up and sniffed: fresh-baked bread. Casseroles had preceded it. He was reminded of the last funeral he'd attended. Mourners can't cook, so you feed them and hope they can eat.

There'd be no funeral in this family; he was sure of that. Ronnie Sue was stuck so full of tubes and needles that he winced when he looked at her, but whatever they were putting in and taking out of her was going to save her.

As for him, he was indeed able to eat, and headed for the kitchen with the gift of bread. The grandparents who weren't at a motel were napping. Billy was wide-eyed, waiting for him.

"Hi, champ. How's it going?" asked Byrne.

Billy didn't answer. The brown eyes turned up to him made him think of spanked puppies and lost souls. Sheila was constantly berating herself for letting the kids out of her sight on Friday evening, but Billy had actually disobeyed orders and led his sister to Mackay's Pond. No one had to punish him; he was suffering terrible remorse.

"Look, kid, I understand how you feel," said his doting uncle. "I think you'll feel better if we go down to the pond again. Like right after we've had some of this nice, fresh bread, okay?"

"I don't want to go," the boy protested.

"I need your help," said Byrne. "We have to trace the woman who pulled Ronnie out."

"Why?"

"Because we need to thank her, sport. She is what's known as a lifesaver."

"The candy?"

41

"No," Byrne said, thinking of how sweet the drenched woman's hair and skin had tasted as he tried to kiss her for comfort.

They ate fistfuls of still-warm French bread, Billy perched on his uncle's knee. Byrne put the little boy up on his shoulders before he headed back to the car.

"We are going to try a reenactment," Byrne said. "We'll do it over again, just what happened on Friday."

Feeling like a film producer, Byrne parked near the junction of the Mackay's Pond lane and the county road and gave Billy instructions. Reluctantly the little boy got out of the car and disappeared down the lane.

Byrne backed up, checked that no other cars were in sight, and touched the horn—their arranged signal. As he eased past the road junction, Billy came running from the direction of Mackay's Pond. He did a great job of acting. Hands out in front of him, the boy flung himself against the side of the car. Byrne braked and got out. Billy knelt on the roadway, squinting up at his uncle.

"Her car was dirty; not clean like yours," said Billy.

"What color was it?" Byrne immediately demanded.

"Blue," he said. "No, maybe green. Dark green."

"Green, huh? That's interesting. What kind of car?" While he interrogated the child, he cursed himself for not having noticed all the cars at the lake when he'd arrived. He hadn't even realized the woman was fleeing before she became only a pair of rapidly departing taillights. Probably she didn't have out-of-state license plates; he would've noticed that.

"I can't tell car makes yet; I'm only seven," Billy said gruffly.

"Right. Okay, you said she put you in the car. Was her car going the same direction as this one is?"

"Yep."

"Heading west then. Next, what was she wear—" Byrne stopped himself. They knew exactly what she wore that Friday night because they still had all her clothing—well, all but her bikini panties. A photographer had snapped a shot of her in that wisp of a garment for the whole nation to ogle, poor kid.

He'd already discovered the photographer's name and chewed him out over the phone for selling the photo to a sensationalistic tabloid. "I coulda sold it to the wire services, too," the guy whined, "but I didn't. I need cash. My wife's pregnant."

"So is Sheila!" Byrne had raged—illogically, since the tabloid story hadn't harmed any of the Coopers. It harmed only the woman who'd saved Ronnie Sue.

"Billy, once she put you in her car," he said, as he hoisted the child into his white Lincoln, "what did you see inside the car? Anything you remember?"

Billy sat and pondered as Byrne drove down the lane approaching the pond. The woman would've hurried, so Byrne stamped on the accelerator.

"You were scared and excited," he went on. "I don't expect you to remember anything much, but did she have something on her dashboard? How about a sticker on a window or something?"

"Sunglasses," he said.

"Where?"

"In a tray, up there." He pointed to the dashboard. "They fell down, but she didn't pick 'em up."

43

"I see. That's a help. You remember the shape or the color of the tray on the dashboard?"

Billy shut his eyes. "Red or purple—I don't know what shape."

They got out of the car. Billy clung to Byrne's leg, the small brown head on a level with Byrne's trouser pocket.

"I told her to go save Ronnie," Billy said. "She told me to go get an ambulance." Then Billy started crying. Byrne picked him up and hugged him.

"You did get help. Twice you got help, Billy. I think you did great. Keep thinking about her car," he added. "Did it have two doors or four?"

"Four," he said after thinking for a moment. "And it was dusty, like you could write your name on it."

"I see." Somehow the idea of the woman driving a dusty, possibly old car was far more intriguing than associating her with a snazzy, shiny 1985 model.

"She had yellow hair," said Billy.

"I beg your pardon?"

"Yellow hair. Like Ronnie's."

"I remember her as brunette—with black or brown hair, Billy."

"But you're asking what I remember."

"I sure am," Byrne said, and then he caught on. Of course! Even the blondest hair turns dark when it's wet.

He drove Billy home slowly and thoughtfully. A blond woman was driving a dusty green car with a red or purple tray on the dashboard, holding sunglasses.

Hendersonville was a city of fewer than seven thousand people. Her telephone call about the tabloid story hadn't sounded like long-distance. She was right here, within reach.

Byrne decided to extend his visit to his North Carolina kinfolk. He had another job to do, now. Besides giving aid to his loved ones, he'd make a survey of automobiles in the city of Hendersonville.

Monday morning Amy drove to work at Blue Ridge Academy, where she ran the main switchboard, connecting calls and furnishing information to inquirers.

What she did not furnish was information about the mystery woman, whom people were busily discussing.

"Why'd she run away?" were the first words Amy overheard. "If *I* did something that great, I'd want to stick around and soak up everyone's praise."

"Did you see the photo of her in the weekly at the supermarket? Wasn't that something?" Ellen blushed as she said this. "And that Cooper guy—what a weirdo! He gets his kicks from hugging a girl who's half frozen to death!"

Amy just kept on plugging and unplugging calls, grateful that she had blond hair and never ran around in a topless bathing suit. Her identity couldn't be discovered if she feigned ignorance and confided in no one.

Would her mother see the tabloid's page one photo of the naked heroine? Way out in California, at last under the protection of a kindly fifth husband, would Mom stare at the photo, then call Fred over and show it to him?

Too bad Mom couldn't know the truth, mused Amy. She'd be pleased, but she was incapable of keeping a secret. The next reporter across Mom's doorstep

45

in Beverly Hills would hear who the mystery rescuer was and sell that information to every tabloid in the country.

Blue Ridge Academy was a church-supported conservative institution which certainly would not appreciate that sort of free publicity, even if it did involve the saving of a child's life.

On her way home from work that evening Amy switched the car radio to a Charlotte station. Even without the newspaper and TV reports, she knew where on the dial she would hear the voice of that man, Byrne Cooper. Tonight she'd worked late so Edythe could have dinner with her kids before coming on switchboard duty. It was already six thirty, about the time she'd pulled Rhonda Sue out of Mackay's Pond, three days ago.

"Good evening," said the same mellow baritone that had recently murmured impassioned thanks into her ear. "This begins a new week of *Conversations with Cooper*. After a message from one of our sponsors, this evening we'll be talking to a physician, a psychologist, and a member of the United States House of Representatives. Topics include recovery from heart attacks and strokes, the effect of Saturday morning TV cartoons on kids, and women in politics."

*Boy*, thought Amy, *you sure hit all the bases, don't you, ol' buddy—medicine, kids, and women all in one evening*. What a relief that the man wasn't going to discuss cold-water drowning, hypothermia, and . . . her.

None of the topics sounded extremely intriguing, but the guests responded eagerly to a man almost as quick and articulate as top network talk-show hosts.

She'd caught Byrne Cooper's show on the infrequent evenings when she was in her car between seven and nine on weekdays.

"An imitation Phil Donahue," she muttered.

She tried not to think of Byrne Cooper's size, his gentle words murmured into her ear. How comforting those words had been, compared to the nasty things he'd told the reporter from the tabloid newspaper. Yes, he had indeed pulled up his sweater to hold her against his chest, but had he done it because it was the best way to warm a hypothermia victim or only for kicks? The contact of his chest and her bosom seemed as recent as five minutes ago to Amy. She flushed, though she'd resisted blushing each time at work she heard discussions going on around her of the mystery woman of Mackay's Pond.

Byrne Cooper had warmed her up and saved her life. Why'd he then have to spoil a kind deed?

The suave, tactful baritone kept eliciting responses from his guests, easing from one to another, bringing up points that the experts missed. Amy cocked her head to catch every word.

When she reached her cabin, empty except for Cornflake and Abercrombie, whom she liked to refer to as her furburgers, she bypassed the TV—for once— and switched on her little-used radio.

She would've preferred to have Byrne Cooper be one of those outrageously obnoxious radio talk-show hosts who succeeded by shocking the public. She wanted to continue to dislike him. For years, however, she'd listened to the man placating paranoiacs and politely getting motormouths off the line, and she'd always pictured him going home to fight with his wife and spank his six kids.

She had not, however, even once heard him refer on the radio to a wife or a child.

## CHAPTER FIVE

Wednesday, on her way home from work at a quarter past five, Amy had only the music on the radio's FM band to listen to. She hoped she wouldn't hear her mom's voice, singing love songs in her husky "whiskey voice." Amy hated the way she was plunged back into helpless childhood each time she heard that voice. The toughest part was its unexpectedness. She never got sufficient warning; rarely did the announcer say, "And now a tune by Evelina Sloan."

Amy always felt false, pretending to Mom that she just loved to hear that familiar voice suddenly burst into song over the radio. Many times in her teen years she'd be enjoying a boyfriend's kiss while his car radio played romantic tunes, and suddenly there was Mom, moaning over lost lovers. Her mother didn't sing any cheerful songs. She sang of betrayal and misery and loss, things with which she was too familiar.

Driving into the countryside this evening, crossing the French Broad—the provocatively named river on which she conducted her rafting trips—Amy started to sing along with the radio. Mom wasn't on.

At home Amy was at last able to hop out of the car instead of stagger. She rejoiced that her full strength at last had returned, before the week was out.

She'd told curious friends at work that she'd been fighting a virus; that's why she was pale and unsure of her footing. No longer. She was in the clear now—permanently anonymous.

She cuddled the pair of fuzzy golden furburgers on the doorstep in the bronze-on-gilt sunset. Then Amy fed them and settled down in front of the television set with a cheese-filled hot dog and a glass of tomato juice. Watching the Olympics for two weeks last summer, conveniently home from work with the flu, she'd gotten addicted to TV. She knew she ought to read more and listen to music, to have friends over and go out on the town, but exciting shows were so accessible, commercials and all. She wasn't going to listen to *Conversations with Cooper* again. It gave her goose bumps.

It was a relief to know that he was back in Charlotte now, not wandering around Hendersonville in search of the missing mermaid whom he'd promised to reward with a demonstration of his sexual prowess—the big oaf!

Suddenly Abercrombie lifted his head and began to bark.

Cornflake went up on tiptoe, ears and tail pointing at the open-beamed ceiling overhead. Amy sprang up. It was past nine, and no one ever came to visit her without telephoning first.

On her way to the door Amy glanced around to make certain that the newspaper and tabloid clippings about the rescue were safely stuck into her photo album and that the ravaged newspaper and tabloid were also out of sight. She'd burned them in her wood stove.

"Who's there?" she asked through the door, one

hand on the safety chain and the other on Abercrombie's ruff as he pressed his body for protection
against her leg while he was growling ferociously.

"Ms. Barrett?" a male voice asked.

Because he said "Ms." and not "Miss," she unlocked the door, but she did not release the chain
holding the door almost shut.

Abercrombie enhanced his ferocious watchdog act,
snarling through the door crack.

"Please, may I talk to you, Ms. Barrett?"

"Who are you, a reporter?" she asked, then realized
that wasn't a smart thing to say. The light over the
front stoop was terribly dim. She couldn't make out
the man's face, but his voice sounded familiar.

"I'm Byrne Cooper," he said. "We've had a terrible
misunderstanding—"

She slammed the door in his face.

Abercrombie barked his approval.

"Don't you want to hear how Ronnie Sue is doing?"
he shouted through the sturdy plank door skewered
with square spikes. She'd built it herself from a "build
your own door" kit.

"Is she okay?" she shouted back, then decided that
that was rude. She cracked the door open again to the
length of the chain.

"How is she?" she asked in a more civilized tone of
voice, trying not to think about the intimate body contact she'd had with this well-known radio personality.

"She's still in a coma. My brother and sister-in-law
are exhausted, keeping vigil. Regardless of your opin-
ion of me, Ms. Barrett, will you please accept our pro-
found gratitude? Will you comfort Mike and Sheila?"

51

"How can I do that?" she asked, suspicious of what this man had in mind.

"For all they know, you're lying dead somewhere at the bottom of a cliff. Without any idea who or where you are—"

"You knew I was okay when I telephoned you. Didn't you tell them about that?"

"I couldn't describe your angry phone call. They'd be stricken if they knew you were justifiably furious. I want them to see you, to meet you in person."

"I don't want the world to know I'm the so-called mystery woman," Amy said, adding, "Hey, how on earth did you find me?"

"Billy described your car. I've been hunting all over town. It was in the academy parking lot."

"It isn't a blue Ford."

"No, it's a dusty green Chevy," he said, a hint of humor in his tone. "Please ask me in. Trust me. I'm harmless, and I didn't make any of those lascivious remarks attributed to me. Haven't you ever been misquoted, Amy?"

*Amy, huh? So we're on a first-name basis,* she silently noted. She pushed the door shut again, but only to unlatch the chain. Then she restrained Abercrombie by his collar. Ten times larger than her cat, he wasn't much stronger than Cornflake. The collie's efforts to "attack" Byrne Cooper would be laughable.

Byrne Cooper came through the door with a loud rustling noise. He was holding over his shoulder three transparent dry cleaner's bags covering garments on hangers.

"My clothes?" Amy asked.

"Yep. Everything's cleaned but your shoes."

Her shoes weighted down the bottom of one plastic bag.

"Well, thanks," she said, embracing the whole bundle. She carried the clothes into the bedroom and laid them on the bed. Her woolens had never looked nicer; she'd never expected to see them again.

The living room, where the man stood, was much too dim. When she hastily switched on another lamp, she got her first good look at Byrne Cooper.

He was staring at her as well.

What a ridiculous reversal of normal events. She'd never even shaken his hand, much less been formally introduced to this man, but they'd embraced, her bare body curled against his, her life in his hands and his arms. Her shiver was impossible to hide.

She tried not to think about what she'd been wearing—rather, what she had *not* been wearing—when he'd pressed her to his bare chest inside his coat. Tonight he was again wearing that same pale sheepskin coat, unbuttoned to show the curly wool lining. She almost reached out to touch it before she stopped her hand from moving. The coat made him look very broad-shouldered. He was also tall, with big brown hands, one of which he extended toward her.

"Shake?" he asked.

She demurred. It was all she could do to look into the dark eyes that examined her—north, south, east, and west. Head bent, brow furrowed, his wide, solemn mouth framed by laugh lines from nose to lips, he awaited some sign of forgiveness.

"I suppose," she said, "I ought to ask you to sit down and offer you coffee."

"That would be very much appreciated," said the tactful host of *Conversations with Cooper.*

Amy couldn't bring herself to suggest he take off his coat. That would only intensify her memories. *Hands off!* she told herself.

Still wearing his coat, he sat down in front of the wood stove. In fact, he sat down so quickly that he almost missed the leather sling chair.

Her collie felt free to rush at Byrne Cooper and kiss him on the cheek. The man was gracious enough not to comment on the behavior of her watchdog, which had been snarling at him only moments ago. Cornflake sat at a distance, her yellow eyes distrustful.

Amy stalked into the kitchen and flipped the gas jet on under the teapot. No brewed coffee for Cooper; he'd have to be content with instant.

"With or without caffeine?" she called out.

"Without, please," he shouted in reply. "The little sleep we get, taking turns sitting with Ronnie Sue at the hospital, is very precious."

Amy remained out of his view till the water was boiling. She put her beige crockery mugs from Pigeon Forge on a round wooden tray with the pewter sugar bowl and creamer. She paused for only a moment before she slid a dozen lemon cookies into a basket and set that on the tray as well.

When she came back into the living room, Byrne Cooper had his chin on his chest, but he wasn't napping; he was staring into the flames visible through the open door of her cast-iron wood stove.

"You've got a wonderfully snug place here," he said. "I couldn't imagine a young woman living alone way out here in a tin-roofed log cabin, but the inside is cozier than my city condo, that's for sure."

"I should hope so," she said, unable to keep the sarcasm out of her voice. "Who decorated your place?"

"I did. I'm not married."

"Oh?"

Her vision of a wife and six kids evaporated.

"Thank you, Amy, if I may call you Amy," he said, lifting his coffee mug and spooning sugar into it. He had trouble inserting his big hand through the handle.

Amy sat down stiffly in the chair to his left. "Well," she began, "I'm waiting for a report on your niece." Then she restated that. "How's the little thing doing?" she asked. "What's her prognosis?"

"It's guarded but very hopeful. They'll soon bring Ronnie out of her coma, since the edema—swelling of her brain—is gone. We take turns talking to her, because her brain waves indicate that she's listening. Experts have flown in from Atlanta and Raleigh. She's getting the best care possible."

"I'm very glad."

"Mike and Sheila will want to give you their heartfelt thanks. They're dying to meet you, Amy."

He kept staring at her. She could feel his gaze, warmer than the fire. "Please," he begged, "let me put their minds at rest. Once they've met you, they can concentrate entirely on Ronnie Sue without any other worry bugging them."

"I don't know," Amy said, regretting the distress she'd inadvertently caused. Ronnie's parents surely bore no blame for what appeared in a tabloid newspaper.

"As for that mendacious article," he said, his chin rising defiantly. "If I meet that so-called journalist for the scandal sheet again, I'll punch his lights out. We refused him an interview, so he said, and I quote, 'If you won't talk to me, then I'll just have to use my imagination.' "

Amy didn't know what to say. As she sipped decaffeinated coffee, she avoided looking at the man whose earnest appeals and magnetic personality threatened her equilibrium. He was now reaching down to pet Abercrombie, who sat on his shoes, leaning against his legs.

"Nice girl," he said. "Nice, fluffy old girl."

"He's a male dog," Amy said.

"Oh, really?" said Byrne Cooper. "At the risk of sounding sexist, I can't imagine an animal this fancy-looking being male."

Instead of feeling offended, she suppressed a smile. "Lassie was a male collie," she said.

"Yep, you're right, and he looked just like this dog. What's her—what's his name?"

"Abercrombie. That's the fanciest name I could think of."

This small talk helped her to relax, to accept his presence in her home, on her turf. Why'd he have to be so handsome and so charming?

"You can discuss breeds of dogs on your next talk show," she suggested, only half joking. "Don't you ever run out of topics?"

"Never. Things pop up hour by hour if I keep my eyes and ears open."

"Are you commuting back and forth to Charlotte, a hundred miles each way?"

"No. The programs this week are on tape. It was just luck that I was here, visiting, when Ronnie almost—" He looked grave, then brightened. "I got compassionate leave so I could stay here and help out the kids."

"Kids?"

"Sheila and Mike. Mike's my younger brother. I'll still be calling them kids when Mike's sixty . . . and I'm sixty-six."

"I see."

Amy needed to say some words that had gone too long unsaid. She'd actually refused to shake the hand or take the coat of the man who'd saved her life.

It would've been so much easier if he'd come here with a wife in tow or with the rest of the Coopers. It would be easier if he were a plumber or a bank teller, if he were plain instead of strikingly attractive. Sensuality surrounded him like an aura, although he behaved like a total gentleman. This man had stripped her and cuddled her; he'd seen and touched her naked body. Why couldn't she laugh it off? She was a big girl now —not a teen-ager or a blushing virgin—but she couldn't help wishing that fate hadn't thrown them together in such a way that they'd begun their acquaintance with instant intimacy.

"Thank you," she whispered, staring into her lap.

"For what?"

"For saving me from dying of hypothermia. It's high time I thanked you."

He laughed out loud. "*I* didn't do anything! Anyone would've done it! That took no brains or courage. *You* were the person with the smarts and the guts last Friday night."

"Well, I—"

"First, you took Billy's word for it that Ronnie was in the pond. Then you went in and found her, pulled her out, in spite of us idiots onshore telling you to give up."

He wasn't finished. She was peeking at him sideways, struck by the animation in his gestures and the way the firelight illuminated his craggy face.

"Then, once she was onshore, *you* demanded she be resuscitated. I don't know what was wrong with the rest of us. We acted like zombies. Hell, the kid was underwater for a quarter of an hour, and we forgot about similar cases—"

He sprang up from his chair, tumbling Abercrombie out of the way.

"Amy," he said, crouching in front of her and capturing both her hands in his. "How many kids die because idiots like me don't dive in to save them and then resuscitate them!"

"I don't know. I guess lots die."

"Let's teach people, then. Look, I've got my own talk show. That can be a start. You'd be a hit on TV—"

"Hey, wait a minute!" Amy said.

"We can turn this whole near tragedy into a force for good, Amy. People everywhere are talking about you and Ronnie Sue, all over America. Think of that! You can use your fame to explain that rescuing drowning people is possible. What attention you'd get!"

"Nope," she said, shaking her head, her eyes on a level with his. She couldn't free her hands from his. He was so close that she could smell his musky masculine scent. Dizzily she imagined him jerking up his sweater and again enclosing her in his coat. Her thoughts were rapidly running back to that anguish-filled Friday night when he'd held her tightly in his arms.

"Hey, you haven't recovered at all. I'm sorry," he said. "You're turning white around the gills. Let's get you down—" He swooped her up in his arms, out of her chair, and carried her to the couch.

"I'm okay!" Amy cried, her struggles no more effective than a pet cat's. The man stretched her out on the burlap-covered couch cushions, stuck one of the needlepoint pillows behind her head, and started chafing her wrists as if he were a gentleman of the Victorian era.

"Have you seen a doctor, Amy?" he demanded.

"Nope. I don't need one. Look, I'm tough," she objected. "I run rafting trips all summer. I know the water. I pull people out all the time!"

That information caused him to hesitate, but only for a moment.

"Where's a thermometer around here?" he demanded. "Your forehead's hot, and your hands feel as cold as ice. I've half a notion to take you to the emergency room."

"Oh, no you don't!" she protested, sitting up.

He shoved her back down on the couch.

"We care about you, you stubborn little rascal!" he shouted in her face. "We love you! You deserve the best in medical care—just what Ronnie herself is getting!"

He knelt by the couch, leaning over her too closely, too warmly, his tan face inches above hers, his sheepskin-clad arms pinning her down. His fingers wandered through the locks of her hair.

"I don't need a doctor," she objected. "I've been back to work all week. I am fine!" She couldn't explain that what caused her pallor, her disorienting excitement, was his nearness. Her brain and heart were replaying the scenario of last Friday night.

"Amy . . ." he said, his dark eyes glowing with compassion and affection.

And then he kissed her.

But it was not a lustful conquest of her lips. He was brushing tender kisses across her forehead from temple to temple. He kissed each of her cheeks, and he was smiling.

"Amy, you gave us back Ronnie—my little niece, Mike's kid. If we'd lost Ronnie, Sheila might've lost the baby she's now carrying, too. Guilt and horror would've consumed every member of our family. Billy still has a lot to overcome as it is. Amy, what sort of reward can we ever give you? What material reward wouldn't be insultingly meager? A thousand bucks? Chicken feed. We want to make you a part of our family. Come home with me tonight, and meet the rest of the family."

She was still in a daze, absorbing this man's warmth and gratitude as if she were his long-lost sister or daughter. No, as if they'd built up a strong relationship and were on the verge of . . . making love. His tenderness and appreciation made her want to weep; he'd wiped away the remnants of her anger.

She sensed that Byrne Cooper longed to kiss her as a man does a woman, full and lingeringly on the lips, but he was restraining himself. He really was not the sort of man who'd say the things attributed to him in the tabloid story. She was grateful for that.

"I'll go to the hospital," she said softly. "But not tonight and not with you. I'll go look in on the child by myself. I've wanted to see her. Please forget about giving me a reward. That's unnecessary and irrelevant. Feeling so happy and . . . yes, so proud of myself is reward enough."

Having said that, she added, "Believe me, I definitely do *not* plan to parade around on TV."

He sat back on his heels. "You sure you feel okay? Your color is better now, but— Why won't you talk about your experience on TV, Amy? It's not difficult or scary. All the questions are gone over in advance."

"Stage fright is only part of the reason I don't want any publicity," she said, managing to sit up, her face still tingling from the touch of his lips. "I've fought a long and bloody battle for my privacy, and I won't give it up now."

"Well, we can discuss that later," he said, not looking at her. She'd heard those words before. It meant she'd won a short reprieve, and then he'd be back at her—with reinforcements.

"Okay, Amy," Byrne went on, still kneeling on the carpet and again seizing her hands. "Are you totally convinced now that I respect you, that I never said those crude things about you?"

She nodded affirmatively.

"You realize that all of us, including Ronnie's grandparents, aunts, uncles, and her eighty-three-year-old great-grandmother as well, want to thank you in person?"

"You *are* going to bring on stage fright now!" she said with a grin.

He checked his watch. "Okay, it's too late tonight; it's almost ten. I won't try to take you anywhere with me now, but I'll be back tomorrow."

"Byr—Mr. Cooper," she said, "Don't let it get around town that I'm the so-called mystery woman, okay? I don't want another spread in the national papers, with or without clothes on. That church-supported school I work for wouldn't appreciate the publicity either."

"I'll try to keep a low profile for you," he said, kneeling on one knee to keep their eyes at the same level. "I'll warn my family not to gossip about their new friend. I'll tell people you're my—my latest lady, okay? And please call me Byrne. Even guests on my show never call me Mr. Cooper."

She lowered her gaze. He sounded so blasted logical. "I'd like to see little Billy again, too," she murmured.

"You will, Amy. Tomorrow. Now, end my curiosity. Why'd you run away from us?" he asked, his eyes alert and curious. "You left your clothes behind and managed to drive away—"

"I didn't like being photographed nude," she said. "And I was zonked out. Hypothermia does that."

"Publicity-shy, huh?" he mused. "That's your right, but in my business it's damnably inconvenient if a person has an important story to tell."

"I meant what I said about maintaining my privacy," she replied in a determined tone of voice.

"Sorry I mentioned it again," he said, lifting her left

hand and gently pressing his lips against the back of it, staring at her over the arc of her bent wrist.

No, Byrne Cooper couldn't come across as anything but sensual. Tonight he'd carried her to the couch and kissed her with the kindest affection, winning her trust, but he hadn't succeeded in playing the role of dear friend or big brother. She'd seen him trying to avoid glancing at her breasts under the blue sweater, and even his kisses, which she was sure were given in the spirit of friendship and gratitude, had seemed imbued with the man's inherent sensuality. She'd never stared into more seductive eyes.

Before she betrayed her feelings, Amy pulled her hands away from the strong, caressing fingers that rubbed them, sending shivers all over her body.

"Well, good night, Amy Barrett," the big man said gruffly. "Be sure to bolt the door behind me. I hate to think of your being all alone here, and that dog"—he indicated the drowsing collie—"wouldn't scare off a mouse."

"I know. He's weak and dumb, but he's a darling."

As Byrne Cooper went out the door, he made his only indiscreet remark of the evening, one that accelerated Amy's heartbeat.

"He's a very lucky collie to live in this charming cabin with you, Amy Barrett."

# CHAPTER SIX

Amy wasn't going to wait till she got off work the next day to go see Ronnie Sue in the hospital. That too-enthralling uncle of Ronnie's would be waiting for her at five, she was sure, and she wanted to sidestep him. One thing at a time. She had an hour off for lunch.

After hopping into her car at eleven-thirty, she drove out of the parking lot without a thought of food. Instead, she headed straight for the medical center.

One week had passed since Ronnie Sue Cooper fell into the pond; it was high time her rescuer had a peek at the little girl. That was the trick: Concentrate on Ronnie and forget the disturbing effect of Ronnie's dashing uncle from Charlotte. He probably had a dozen women on the string. His affection for her might spring only from gratitude—gratitude mixed with embarrassment over being misquoted in a sleazy tabloid.

*But why am I primping up for a comatose child?* Amy asked herself in the hospital parking lot. She'd adjusted her rearview mirror to guide her in repairing her lipstick and mascara and combing her hair. She wore dark green pants and a tan turtleneck sweater. These colors made her hair glow golden.

Reaching the intensive care unit, Amy glanced

around with the anxious caution of a spy on the prowl. A sign on the door said IMMEDIATE FAMILY ONLY.

*I guess that doesn't mean me,* Amy thought, and sighed. Then it occurred to her that Byrne had dubbed her an honorary family member. She had no family east of California and had never deceived herself that her half brothers and sisters were close friends of hers. She and her mother were close, but their visits and even phone calls exhausted Amy emotionally.

At the station outside the double doors to intensive care sat a graduate of the academy where Amy worked. What luck. Their eyes met, and the freckled red-haired nurse said in an excited but soft voice, "Amy Barrett! It's been years! You're lookin' so good!"

"Cecelia, you *did* become a nurse, then!"

"Yep, and I love it. Hey, it's good to see you, again, Amy. You still rafting on the river?"

"Yes, but right now I need help in getting through those doors. Think you can sneak me in?"

"Which patient do you want to see?"

Amy took a deep breath. "Rhonda Sue Cooper." She said those three words and no more. Prattling would be dangerous. Cecelia gave her a conspiratorial wink, checked to see if anyone was in sight, and then led the way into ICU.

"I don't blame you," the nurse whispered, "she's gotten so famous. No wonder you're interested, taking all those folks out on the river. I'll go in with you for a moment."

Never once in six years in Hendersonville had Amy been admitted through these doors. She'd had friends who landed in intensive care, but no family members.

65

"There she is, the dear little thing," Cecelia whispered, pointing.

They stood in a hexagonal carpeted room containing several staff desks. The six walls surrounding them were all glass, allowing them to look right into six small rooms. In half the rooms white-draped patients lay still and silent among hanging bottles and shining machinery with dials and levers. The only colors visible were the chrome fittings of the respirators, electrocardiograms, and bed tables and the pastel hues of solutions in the intravenous bottles.

The smallest patient by far was Ronnie Sue Cooper.

In her dim room a curly blond head lay on a flat pillow. A young woman was visible from the waist up, seated beside the bed. Tubes and wires radiated from the small patient. Amy's various paramedical courses had taught her their functions—monitoring brain waves and heart function, supplying oxygen and nutrition, among other things.

"The family is super. At least one of them is here every minute, day and night, watching over Ronnie and talking to her," said Cecelia.

"That's her mother," murmured Amy, breathing more and more quickly. Sheila Cooper had been her collaborator in the rescue. She'd screamed for Ronnie to be resuscitated when Amy was hypothermic and fainting, her voice only a fading squeak.

"Sometimes it's the uncle, that Byrne Cooper, the big hunk who has the radio show out of Charlotte," murmured Cecelia.

"How is Ronnie?" asked Amy, hiding her wince.

"She nods and shakes her head to questions," the nurse said. "She's still on phenobarb and the respirator, but she hasn't got a stomach ulcer, like some kids get."

"An ulcer?" Amy asked, visualizing harried business executives sipping antacids.

"In the coma she isn't under so much stress. I tried to read up on cases like hers, but there's not much published yet, even in the hospital library."

Again Amy winced. If doctors and nurses lacked data about kids like Ronnie, how much less did the public know? If she herself hadn't asked questions about drowning in an emergency medical techniques class—

The mother stood up, gazed for a moment down at Ronnie, and then came toward them.

Amy turned casually toward a chart rack, saying, "Could I glance at her chart?"

Sheila Cooper passed by, murmuring in a soft, sweet voice, "I'm going to grab a snack in the coffee shop, okay? I won't be more than ten minutes."

"I'll watch over Ronnie," said Cecelia as Amy, her back to Sheila, flipped through the chart. The atrocious handwriting communicated little.

When Sheila was gone, Amy followed her nurse friend into Ronnie Sue's room, tiptoeing, grimacing with nervous expectation. Cecelia sat down in the chair close by the bed, and Amy gazed at the child.

She was in a drug-induced coma, just sleeping. She was not dead. What a miracle! Tears filled Amy's eyes, and she didn't try to hide them. Anyone would weep to see this four-year-old cherub who'd lain for a quarter of an hour or more on the muddy bottom of an icy, murky pond, given up for dead.

One small arm—pink, no longer blue—was taped to

a board, and a tube went into a vein. A tube was taped to her nose for oxygen. She moved her rosebud lips, and Cecelia hastened to moisten them with something on a cotton swab. Long lashes shadowed Ronnie's cheeks . . . and fluttered.

Amy wanted to cry, to cry out, rejoicing. Her heart swelled enormously inside her, pulsing. She felt like an Olympic world champion, a Nobel prizewinner, and Miss America rolled into one. She'd done this, made this possible, she and no one else. Billy had been essential, Sheila had been essential, but Amy Barrett had used her head and risked her own life to save this little child.

She'd always heard that conceit is bad and pride is evil. The pride she was feeling right now, however, was not an evil thing. By saving Ronnie she'd made up for faults she had and people she'd inadvertently hurt. Yes, she did deserve praise—her own praise. She did feel proud of her deed. No one needed to thank or reward her. Her own inner gratification would last a lifetime.

Cecelia missed seeing the parade of emotions crossing Amy's rapt face. Ronnie Sue suddenly moved her free hand on the white sheet, made a fist, and then opened her tiny fingers.

"May I touch her?" Amy whispered.

Cecelia nodded.

The distance across the covers to that little pink daisy of a hand seemed a mile. Amy reached forward very slowly, her fingers curved and poised; she lightly stroked the dimpled back of Ronnie's hand. Her heart jolted. So precious! Fully alive! Warm and alive, Ronnie was lying here resting, thinking things over. Amy wanted to say, "Hey, remember me? We met at the bottom of a pond. I didn't touch you with exquisite gentleness then, sweetheart, did I? I grabbed you and yanked you to the surface and practically threw you toward shore, remember?"

Amy blinked hard, withdrawing her hand. Ronnie Sue sighed. Seeing and touching her were reward enough. Seeing this child was like food and drink to a starving person. Amy wallowed in happiness. Someday she'd find an opportunity to hold and hug Ronnie Sue, when she was out of the hospital, all healed, all well.

"I'd better go. I don't want to give her any germs," Amy whispered.

"It isn't sterile in here. That huge family all comes in, except her brother, who's too young to be admitted."

Amy left anyway, looking back to see Cecelia adjust a dangling tube, turn a dial, and tidy the bedside tray.

In the central area Amy's eyes again sought the bit of Ronnie Sue's face visible through the window. A shadow passed her—Sheila Cooper, already back, carrying a styrofoam cup and a candy bar. She and Cecelia changed places at the bedside.

Amy couldn't take her eyes off the little girl. She didn't look around when Cecelia rested a gentle hand on her shoulder. Touched by this affectionate companionship, she reached up to squeeze Cecelia's hand.

The fingers she touched were thick, hard, and rough.

Amy spun around.

It wasn't Cecelia after all. Byrne Cooper had come

up beside her, his smile appearing over Amy's shoulder. He gave her a friendly one-armed hug.

"Hello, Amy," he said softly. "What do you think of our Ronnie?"

"She looks wonderful," Amy said.

His slight nod reassured her before his words did. He calmly asked, "You two know each other?"

Cecelia explained that she used to hang around the school switchboard when Amy was on duty. Then Cecelia, flushing and stammering, fled back through the double doors.

"Want to meet Sheila now, Amy?" Byrne asked quietly.

"I'd better rush back to work," Amy said.

"I suppose this evening would be a more appropriate time," he agreed. "We have to maintain quiet and calm in a hospital."

Instead of his sheepskin coat, today he wore a dark blue business suit over a white-collared pale blue shirt. Amy wondered if every outfit this man wore looked devastating on him. He accompanied her out of the intensive care unit and down the hall.

When Amy explained, "My friend slipped me in," he halted and boxed her in against a wall.

"Who on earth has more right than you to visit Ronnie?" he whispered, sounding almost angry. His dark eyes glinted.

"When Ronnie wakes up, she'll want to see her parents' faces. I'm a total stranger to her."

Of course, this wasn't what he'd meant at all. He wasn't talking about practicality; he was talking about her moral right, the idealist!

Down in the parking lot Byrne said, "I'll pick you

70

up at five, okay? Your true identity won't keep any longer than that."

"Make it ten after."

"Okay, ten past five, at the academy," he said, smiling at her fondly.

Amy got into her car, the one Billy had identified, thinking about the Coopers. What a devoted family. Why hadn't she been blessed with a loving family when she herself was a yellow-haired four-year-old?

She felt tempted to leave work before five, to flee again just to avoid the great revelation scene. Why? She did deserve thanks, and they deserved to quit worrying about her welfare.

One problem was this identity thing—or rather her mother's identity. Hendersonville was a quiet, conservative community; that's why she liked it here. *The reputation of a parent rubs off on a child, face it,* she told herself. Daughters are expected to be a lot like their mothers, but she wasn't one bit like Evelina Sloan. And she didn't want some astute reporter to make the connection between the famous singer whose long battle with alcoholism and five marriages had been chronicled in the nation's tabloids and the mild-mannered switchboard operator at Blue Ridge Academy. She'd fought her way out of the limelight and wasn't going to let herself be thrown back in just because she'd done a good deed.

Another problem was Byrne Cooper. *C'mon, admit it,* she told herself. *He captivates you.* If only he'd go back home to Charlotte before she fell into the loving arms of the Cooper family, before she waded into their lives and found herself in over her head.

## CHAPTER SEVEN

Byrne cursed himself for allowing Sheila to brood about Amy for five more hours. In the hospital he could have said, "Here's Amy, the woman who rescued Ronnie." Sheila must have seen Amy without suspecting anything. And Byrne would probably have introduced the two women right then and there if Amy's haunted eyes hadn't told him that she dreaded revealing her identity as the mystery woman. Why was she so modest, so reluctant to own up to having risked her own life to save a drowning child? he wondered. The woman was a true hero and deserved to be hailed as one.

He'd go crazy, counting off the minutes until five, when he could pick Amy up at work. When Mike arrived at the hospital to replace Sheila, he had driven her home, where she collapsed into a nap. Together her mother and father got dinner in the oven. His and Mike's parents were staying at a motel nearby, having flown in from Richmond with his grandmother. A big family dinner was planned tonight to give everyone a relief from the tension and anxiety that had plagued their lives since last Friday night. What a great setting for them to meet Amy in and deluge her with gratitude, he thought.

"Let's have a special-duty nurse with Ronnie for just an hour or two tonight, Sheila," he and Mike had pleaded. "It's been a whole week. You deserve an uninterrupted sit-down meal with your family. You'll crack up."

Byrne had hugged them both. It was just his style to be warm and affectionate with people he liked and loved. He was a demonstrative man. He'd hugged Amy Barrett alive last Friday night, and yesterday he'd carried her to her couch, laid her down, and kissed her. He hoped she'd received his kisses as affectionate gratitude, nothing more. He certainly didn't want to scare her off. But he couldn't deny the passionate and very manly desires that that lovely, shy, gentle woman awakened in him.

On Friday night, horror and dread had obsessed him, distracting him from the fact that the woman whose life he was preserving was a hell of a good-looking desirable female . . . and practically naked. On Wednesday he had wanted to make love to her right on that couch, but he couldn't let her suspect that. She was too frightened of him to look him in the eyes. Obviously she was shy and didn't appear to enjoy having a lot of contact with people. Extroverts didn't live with two animals out in the woods and run rafting trips and operate switchboards.

When he and Billy located her car in the academy's parking lot yesterday, he'd felt like leaping—or weeping—with joy. Billy was excited, too. His success had finally cheered him up.

Byrne had once done a talk show on sibling rivalries. He wasn't surprised when the sad little boy confided, "I didn't push my sister in! I didn't! I like Ronnie! She slipped and fell in."

"No one's imagined you harmed Ronnie," he'd assured the boy, and hugged him fiercely. Then he'd given Billy the thrill of pursuing Amy when she left work. From 4:00 to 5:00 P.M., they'd sat in the parking lot, waiting to see who left the campus and got into that green Chevy. When the tall, slim young blond woman appeared, he and Billy both had recognized her. She was the one! Then he and Billy, TV detective-style, had shadowed her car on its meandering journey out into the country, across the French Broad River. He noted the location of her rural mailbox and the private lane that led into the riverside woods.

He'd pledged Billy to secrecy, driven him home, and then gone back alone at night to confront Amy.

His and Billy's secret surely couldn't keep more than twenty-four hours. Leaving Sheila and her folks at home, he ferried his own folks and his grandmother from their motel to the house and then picked up Billy at afternoon Bible school at four.

History was repeating itself. Just as they had yesterday at this hour, they sat in the academy parking lot watching the green Chevy. Byrne couldn't stand it.

"Look, let's go in and get her. I know where she is; she runs the switchboard."

"Can I come, too?"

"Sure you can, buster! After all, you're the one who found her."

Amy turned her head in shock. Two sets of small fingers were creeping over the edge of the high counter

74

that separated her switchboard from the entrance to the academy office.

She'd seen something like that in a recent movie. What had appeared was the adorable gremlin called Gizmo. This was no gremlin. With a scramble of feet a little boy pulled himself up so his hair and eyes appeared over the counter.

She knew those eyes.

"Billy!"

She sprang up and ran around the end of the counter, leaving the switchboard buzzing behind her. She scooped up Billy Cooper.

"How'd you get here all alone?" she asked, afraid he was running away from home. Was he still racked with guilt over taking Ronnie to Mackay's Pond?

"Uncle Byrne's here," he said, pointing out the door.

Of course, she might have guessed. Here came Byrne Cooper, grinning from ear to ear.

"You off duty yet?" he greeted her, checking his watch. "We couldn't wait, Billy and I."

She was kissing Billy. "You deserve a prize," she told the little boy. "You saved your sister's life."

"I didn't. *You* did."

"Okay, we did."

"One down and seven to go," said Byrne. "You've got to meet all the rest of the family."

"Seven more?" she gasped.

"It'll be nine, counting Billy and me. C'mon, beautiful Amy." He touched her arm, which was looped around Billy. His eyes were glowing, full of gratitude . . . or was it more?

"I can't leave till my replacement arrives," Amy

said, leading Billy around the counter to see the lights flashing on her switchboard. She connected and disconnected several calls, then leaned back, stretching out her cramped back. Sitting was the worst position in which to spend a day. Her stomach growled; she'd skipped lunch to go visit Ronnie.

Nothing she could think about, however, took her mind off the man who leaned his elbows on the counter, watching her intently.

"Was the water real cold?" asked Billy.

Amy did a momentary double take. No one was in the office listening. "Oh, the pond. Yes, it was awfully cold. That was lucky for Ronnie. It preserved her."

"Like jelly preserves?"

"No, like—like a Popsicle."

"She hasn't woken up yet."

"I know, Billy. It's good for her to rest a little while longer. You'll have to tell her everything that's happened while she's been asleep," Amy whispered, afraid she was going to cry. Billy's voice was plaintive; his eyes—dark like Byrne's—were hungry for assurance. No, Ronnie wasn't dead; yes, he was a good boy. *We all make mistakes,* she wanted to say. She'd dreamed of running away from home all through her childhood, and during several of her Mother's comas, she'd wished Mom would never wake up. Faithfully writing home and visiting didn't remove all of one's childhood guilts.

She had no more leisure to hug or to converse. Calls were coming into the office, and so were professors and students. Byrne stepped back and leaned against the wall, with Billy beside him. They watched Amy at work. That she fumbled and stumbled was probably not obvious to them, and people who didn't know her might mistake the big, handsome man for her husband and Billy for her own little son.

Amy kept her word. She got into her Chevy and followed Byrne Cooper's Lincoln through town and back into the suburbs. She winced when she turned left at a signpost that read ORCHARD LANE.

On the brick path up to the brick house she felt like Dorothy in *The Wizard of Oz*. Billy was holding her hand, and Byrne walked so close behind her that she could feel him. At the steps he closed his hand around her upper arm—like a cop with a prisoner. She did need steadying.

Billy shoved the door open on a comfortable red-carpeted living room with floral upholstery and a fireplace. The fragrance of roasting beef activated hunger pains in Amy's stomach.

Little Billy opened his mouth and yelled, "Mama! It's *her!*"

"Who?" An elderly man entered the room, wearing an oven mitt on his hand. Two white-haired women appeared behind him.

Amy glanced up at Byrne, who grinned like the cat who'd just swallowed the canary.

Not sure who the three elderly people were, Amy did recognize Sheila, who came staggering from the hallway, barefoot, trying to smooth down her mussed hair.

"What'd you say, Billy?" she asked.

"The lady! The lady who rescued Ronnie!"

"Oh, my God!" exclaimed the old man.

"It's the one from the hospital," Sheila whispered, still in the process of waking up.

The front door flew open again, and a tall, dark man entered, breathless.

"That's the car!" he said excitedly. "The one we're search—"

"And this is the woman," Byrne said, his arm around Amy's shoulders.

Sheila burst into tears.

From somewhere else in the house a couple who must have been in their early sixties appeared, the man in suspenders. "What's going on?" the woman asked.

"Byrne's found—Billy's found—the rescuer!"

Before Amy could speak or move, like a magnet dropped among metal shavings, she drew everyone in the room into a noisy collision with her. Arms embraced her from waist to neck. People kissed her on the cheeks, on the hair. Someone captured her hand and kissed the back of it.

Amy was weeping now, too.

"Let her breathe!" came Byrne's unmistakable radio personality's voice.

Amy was half carried to the couch and eased down into the very middle of it. A grandmother—certainly a grandmother—leaned against her, gripping her hand. Sheila sat on the other side of her, and Mike Cooper actually knelt at her feet, the way Byrne had the night before.

"You angel!" one of the grandmothers kept saying. "You wonderful angel."

"She was so brave. She dived into that icy water," the oldest woman said, shaking her head. Byrne stuck a rocker under her and sat her down so she looked like Whistler's mother.

"I'm Ruby Cooper, Ronnie's great-grandmother,"

she told Amy. "I thank you, young lady. Thank you, thank you, thank you."

"But I didn't— Anyone would've— Please, I'm getting embarrassed—" she pleaded, but through her tears she was smiling.

They were overdoing it, but so many people—nine of them?—couldn't all be wrong. They thanked her and hugged her and kissed her over and over again.

"The roast will burn!" someone said, and ran out of the room.

"You'll eat with us," said Mike, his pleasant face younger than Byrne's and more rounded, less striking. "What can we ever do to repay you?" He glanced up at his brother. "What's her name? I didn't even catch her name!"

"Amy," said one grandmother. "She's named Amy. Amy what? Was it Barnett?"

Someone left and came back with a big box of tissues. Hands grabbed for them and wiped eyes and noses. A granddad handed her a tissue.

Sheila, standing beside her husband, said, "There's nothing we can give you that'll express half our—one-millionth of what we feel about you, Amy." She looked hopefully around the room. "You're a member of this family now. You're Ronnie's godmother automatically. I can't talk. I can't express myself at all," she said, breaking into a sob.

"You're wonderful," said Amy, and everyone was instantly silent to listen to her. That was as great a compliment as being hugged and kissed.

"I don't really have any family," she confided, and because everyone gazed at her adoringly, she said more than she should have. "I never had a real sister or brother, or even a dad around, and my mom was . . . troubled. This is—is Christmas to me."

Sheila Cooper moved closer, seized Amy's hand, and pressed it against her swelling abdomen. "If this baby is a girl, her name is going to be Amy." It might have been too melodramatic, if anyone else said it, even if it were a line in a play, but Sheila had put her heart into the words.

The room was silent. Amy broke the silence with a sniffle of gratitude. "That is so sweet. . . ."

"If it's a boy," said Mike, "how about Barrett? Barrett Cooper?"

"That's going a little too far." Amy giggled, breaking the tension. Some of them chuckled.

"I'm hungry," said Billy.

"I'm hungry, too," Amy agreed. "Breakfast was my last meal."

"Feed her!" shouted Great-grandma from her rocker. "Get in there, and get this girl some grub!"

## CHAPTER EIGHT

The meal was a feast—a love feast as well as a banquet for a starving woman. As she ate the good food, seated among these attentive, affectionate people, Amy for the first time admitted to herself, *I've been deprived all my life of a family.* A good thing that she hadn't discovered this fact before now; it might have led to self-pity, which she detested.

Every word that one of the Coopers or Sheila's parents said to her made Amy feel precious and loved. It was embarrassing, but it certainly felt good.

How different she'd feel if she'd met Byrne Cooper under more normal circumstances and come home with him to dinner. Visiting other guys' families had always been an ordeal, at least at first. *Will they like me? Approve of me?* she'd always asked herself. *Will I like them?* Tonight she sure didn't have to ask any such questions. As far as liking his family, this was like the big Thanksgiving dinners she'd seen on touching TV commercials—from great-grandma to the kids.

Pretty soon, she hoped, there'd be two kids at the table, not just one . . . and baby would make three.

After the roast beef, baked potatoes, glazed carrots, lima beans, Jello-O salad, and chocolate cake, she offered to help do dishes. Everyone hooted at her.

*"You?* Do dishes? Are you *CRAZY?"*

It might as well have been Queen Elizabeth who was offering to help out in the kitchen.

Amy found herself escorted back to the living room and plunked down knee to knee with Sheila, who never seemed to take her eyes off Amy's face.

Amy sighed. "I feel like . . . Every time you look at me, Sheila, you sort of pick your heart up off the floor."

"That *is* the way it feels, Amy. I wish we had a million dollars to give you. I really do."

"A million bucks is nothing," said Amy, who knew what she was talking about. "What I've found in this house"—she had to pause for a beat to regain control of her voice—"is worth—worth ten million dollars."

What she didn't tell them was that her own mother had earned tens of millions of dollars by now—and spent it. The old saying about money's not buying happiness was true in her and her mother's case. An abundance of cash had not brought them joy. It had brought reporters and agents to their doorstep, along with countless freeloaders, panderers, con men, and con women. Men who referred to themselves as business managers tried to "package" Evelina's blond and pretty teen-age daughter as a rock singer, though Amy had no musical talent. When one guy tried to seduce Amy into going onstage, her mother had punched him out.

The TV and nightclub entertainers in her mother's league who were rich and famous but who also happened to be nice people, couldn't put up with Evelina for long. Her close buddies were people like her who overused pills, alcohol, and sex for comfort. Right out of high school Amy had fled, first to the wholesome corn belt and then further east.

She was certainly glad today that she'd chosen this particular haven nestled in the North Carolina mountains.

Byrne Cooper had sat close beside her at dinner and remained within reach. She'd feel his hand on her shoulder or a finger tipping her chin up so he could smile into her face. He'd gallantly helped her out of one chair and eased her into another, and when she was standing, he'd been right there, looping an arm around her shoulders.

Amy found she had a very high tolerance for attention. She hadn't been dating anyone this year, her partner in the rafting business, Irene, hadn't arrived for the summer, and there were limits to the conversational abilities of a collie and a pussy cat.

"You are making one terrific impression; notice that, Amy?" asked Byrne, murmuring into her ear as he sat beside her on the couch.

Sheila broke in with a question. "Why'd you wait so long to tell us who saved Ronnie?" she asked her brother-in-law. "She was at the hospital, early this afternoon, Byrnie."

"The hospital is a lousy place for a big introduction scene," he said.

"My brother," Mike put in, "is always directing scenes and producing dramas. He's always on the job, Amy."

"So I've noticed."

Byrne looked crestfallen. "Hey, that's not fair," he objected. "I kept quiet because I was afraid of your reaction, Sheila, and I knew Amy was scared stiff, she's so publicity-shy."

"You wanted the largest possible audience," Mike said, correcting his brother. "The whole family had to meet her all at once. Well, you sure got what you aimed for."

Hearing his brother and sister-in-law chiding Byrne, sensing a trace of good-natured sibling rivalry here, Amy opened her mouth to defend Byrne. She shut it again when Byrne said, "I'm trying to persuade Amy to go on radio and TV with her story, hers and Ronnie's. Maybe Billy can be featured as well as the two of you." Byrne looked at Sheila and Mike. "Amy, however, would be the big draw; she'd wow 'em, being famous already nationwide."

"There he goes again!" Sheila's mother remarked. "Byrne never tires of looking for new radio show ideas."

"Well, he makes a heap of money doing things his way," Byrne's father pointed out.

"I don't like the idea of reminding people how they showed poor Amy in the newspaper," Byrne's mother mumbled to herself—a little too audibly.

Seeing that everyone was visualizing the photo of her nearly nude, Amy felt her face grow hot. Each member of the family reacted differently to her blush. Mike Cooper dropped his gaze, Sheila shook her head in commiseration, but both grandfathers hid smiles and lifted eyebrows, indicating that they weren't yet in their dotage.

Ronnie's irrepressible great-grandmother blurted out, "Don't you blush, girl! You've got a darned nice figure, and you shouldn't be ashamed of it."

"I—I'm not," Amy said, restoring their composure. "I'm sure Byrne will figure out a way to inform the public about resuscitation without featuring me. Once Ronnie's back to normal, she'd make a big hit on TV —if her parents approve, that is."

Byrne didn't comment. He sent Amy a calculating glance that sizzled across the room and made her remember kissing him.

Amy stayed at the Cooper house until Sheila and her father left for the hospital and then telephoned home to report that Ronnie hadn't roused during the two hours they'd all been absent. The brief family holiday that restored some equilibrium to rattled psyches had done Ronnie no harm.

"It's a good thing the grandparents are retired and can stay here to help out," said Byrne, fetching Amy's coat. "Sheila's brothers just left; it's too bad they missed meeting you. The hospital approved all of us as immediate family, and you'll pass muster as well, Amy."

"Good," she said. "I want to watch Ronnie's progress."

When she disentangled herself from Byrne's kinfolk and stepped out the door, Byrne said, "I'm following your car, Amy. I don't like your driving home so late alone."

"I've lived there for the past six years," she said, "and nothing's happened to me. Sometimes hunters or picnickers politely ask to cross my property. I'm safer even than in town."

Of course, arguing wouldn't convince him. Byrne wasn't thinking logically. He was obsessed with keeping her safe, making her happy, rewarding her. That was fine with Amy, just so long as her mother didn't get dragged into the picture.

Imagine what the people in that house would think of torch singing in nightclubs, five husbands, alcoholism, and drugs. Amy had noted that a plaque with a psalm hung on their kitchen wall, and a Bible lay on a table. Amy had bowed her head before dinner while Mike said a long grace, thanking God for having sent her to rescue Ronnie. No one smoked in that house, no liquor was served, and only Great-grandma cussed.

When both cars arrived at the end of her private lane, Byrne didn't ask permission to get out of his car and come into the house with her. As Amy unlocked her front door, he stood right beside her, patting Abercrombie, the collie.

"I'll remember tonight forever," he said, using the exact words she was about to say. "I hope you felt all the love and gratitude flowing in your direction."

"Felt it flowing? It was a tidal wave! I was drowning —but I loved it. Four generations making over me at once! I felt like a queen."

"No queen I ever heard of dived into ice water after a kid. That's a poor comparison. How about a saint?"

A saint? Amy had turned on her car radio to keep her awake, driving home, and her mother's voice had blared out of the speakers and coiled itself around the car, throatily murmuring about lost loves and hot passion. No way could Amy forget her mother for long; Evelina Sloan records were too popular.

Diamonds glittering, silk loungewear rustling, Evelina rose up like a ghost in Amy's mind, standing there, giving orders to the cook and the maid, a cigarette hanging out of one corner of her mouth. *Not exactly a childhood that would breed a saint,* Amy thought.

At least Mom had done some things right. When Amy was ten, her mother had handed her a cigarette to puff on, hoping it would be unpleasant. It was. Amy choked so badly that she had little trouble in her teens resisting peer pressure to take up smoking. Thanks to her mother, it held no romantic appeal for her.

"And don't you *ever* let me catch you taking pills!" Mom had stormed. "Aspirin only—that is *it!* You hear me? Do what I say do; don't do as I do. You want to get all wrinkled and lined, so you have to get your face lifted but still lose your husbands to younger women?"

Amy closed her eyes tightly in an effort to wipe away the painful memories and vowed to avoid music stations at all costs. Being reminded of her mother unsettled her deeply and disrupted the personal tranquillity she'd been working hard to achieve since she'd come to the Carolina mountains. From now on she'd listen to Byrne's talk show. It would help her get to know this intriguing man with the idyllic family a lot better. She had to be kidding herself. The man stood right on her doorstep. She could get to know him a heck of a lot better, in a much more exciting way, this very night.

## CHAPTER NINE

Once they were inside her log cabin, Amy offered Byrne a glass of wine. She was surprised but not displeased when he said, "Nope, I don't know if I'm staying long enough to absorb it before I drive home. I just hosted a panel on 'drink driving'—the term Europeans find more useful than our term, 'drunk driving.' "

"That's an interesting point," she said, much impressed. "Your shows are really oriented toward public service, aren't they?"

"You missed all those discussions of sin and sex?" he said. "Don't get the impression that I'm as staid as my brother. I'm on my best behavior in Hendersonville." He rolled his eyes heavenward. "I've had guests discussing sexual options and pornography, and occasionally I interview sex therapists and controversial rock stars."

"Ummm-hmmm, I've heard some of those shows," she said. "I've become a fan. I listened even before I met you, and now my poor ol' TV set is going to get jealous."

"I'll be moving to TV in June," he said. "Someone finally decided that my hair was thick enough and my waist still slim enough—" He interrupted himself. "Let's not talk about my show. I'll be back to work soon enough, as it is. How about a kiss?" he added. "A good night kiss."

Amy assessed him carefully. If he'd gone ahead and kissed her, she wouldn't have struggled, but his request required a considered reply.

He didn't give her much time to ponder, however. He opened his arms, she went into them, and the kiss they shared wasn't expressive merely of gratitude or friendship. The husky, dark-browed, good-smelling man really got down to business. Her happiness at seeing Ronnie and spending an evening in the bosom of the Cooper family made Amy fling her arms around Byrne's neck and hold tight, welcoming his seeking lips and teasing tongue.

Amy entered a new realm with Byrne Cooper. Her fiancé, whom she'd ditched after he'd hit her, had kissed her awkwardly and roughly. Byrne Cooper knew how to begin slowly and make her long for more —for more pressure, more penetration, more nearness. Yes, and long for less clothing between their bodies. Tonight, five or six layers of fabric separated them, and her breasts, which remembered the warmth of his chest, ached at being in contact with Byrne again. Her body recognized his. After all, his body had warmed hers back to life.

Gracefully Byrne managed to shed his suit coat and pull her jacket off her.

"Remember the Chinese proverb?" he said. "One is responsible all one's life for a person whose life one has saved."

"So I'd better watch over Ronnie Sue very carefully," she said, hiding a smile; he hadn't been talking about Ronnie Sue this time.

"Amy Barrett, you are the one I am responsible for."

Fine. She was already an honorary member of this man's family. They'd been acquainted for a week and had begun their relationship with an even warmer embrace than this one.

He continued to nibble on Amy's lips and draw her tongue tip into his mouth, caressing her back, his big, powerful hands moving in circles over her sweater. She loved his touch, and while it excited her, stirring her desire and making her feel very much a woman, it also made her feel safe and secure, cherished and protected. She trusted him. He'd saved her, yes, and he sprang from such solid, wholesome stock.

As Byrne eased her toward the couch where last night he'd hovered over her like an attending physician, Amy remembered the question to which she needed a true, totally believable answer.

"You know, you're a very attractive, dashing character, Byrne Cooper. Even your name has a ring to it. Are you really and truly unmarried? Honest to goodness?"

He gave a short, incredulous laugh. "Amy, remember tonight at Mike's house? Do you actually think I could get away with falling all over an attractive woman like you in front of Mike, Sheila, her family, plus my own mother and father, *and* that old spitfire my grandmother if I were married? Come on, now!"

"I'm too happy, I guess, to think straight," she said, smiling as she stroked the tanned, clean-shaved sides of his face. "I got the impression that your grandma's the biggest rascal in the whole family. All of them are

90

darlings, but Grandma! It'd take a lot to shock her, wouldn't it?"

"She's old enough to get away with murder," he said. "Thank you for liking them. And you should've heard what they said about you when you weren't listening."

"That bad?" she said only half teasingly.

"You would've blushed to hear! No, seriously. I think if they could adopt you, they would. You're now thought of as Ronnie's godmother, Sheila's only sister, and a new granddaughter."

"I can't think of a greater reward," Amy said, shutting out the twin images of her nude photo in the tabloid and her notorious mother in California.

He sat down on the couch and pulled Amy onto his lap. He pulled off her boots one by one.

"I seem to remember doing this last week," he murmured as he dropped one boot after the other on the carpet.

"But you're going to stop right there," she told him, unable to keep from smiling.

Byrne lifted a brow. "Oh, yeah?" he said, low in his throat. "Are you actually going to try to stop me?" He kissed the side of her mouth. "You'd stop a man who's thirty-four years old, still single, and never before more glad of that fact?"

"I'm glad I'm single, too. I almost ended up a battered bride," Amy confided in turn. "I found out just in time."

"Thank God!" he said earnestly. "And you're still shy of men, I daresay."

"It takes a while for me to trust people, yes."

"Do you trust me, Amy?" he asked softly.

"Just drop your campaign to put me on television, Byrne. Aside from your pushiness about that, well . . ." She looked directly into his eyes. "I do like you," she concluded.

"I'll cool it," he said, "for a while. On some rare occasions I do manage to put pleasure ahead of business, Amy Barrett."

"I'm glad to hear that."

They spent the next ten minutes tasting and tantalizing each other's lips, Amy reclining in his arms, across his lap, her head nestled into his shoulder. Unconsciously they'd resumed the posture in which he'd held her on Friday night, except that she was clothed.

Watching Amy's eyes intently, Byrne began to slide his hand up under her sweater, stroking her bare back, his thumb counting her ribs without tickling. He was a very skillful lover. His dark brows rose momentarily when he discovered she wasn't wearing a bra.

She often didn't wear one and felt she didn't need one under sweaters this thick or blouses with front pockets.

"You know," he said, "maybe this will insult you, Amy, but I really didn't think about you sexually on Friday evening. It was a life-or-death matter for two lovely girls."

"You didn't even notice whether I was male or female?" she asked, cocking a brow and suppressing a grin.

"I wouldn't go so far as to say *that,*" he said, inching his hand forward below her raised arm to the swell of her left breast. His hand halted.

"That's why that damned article burned me up," he explained. "It wasn't till after I read it that I really understood how sensual our—our situation was that night. The public got titillated reading about it. To tell the truth, reading what I supposedly said turned *me* on. That photo of you didn't help either. I kept telling myself you were most likely a mother—a married woman, totally unavailable, or someone just passing through town whom I'd never find again."

His hand cautiously covered her breast, forcing a gasp past her lips. He could recognize her own excitement in the stiffening of her nipple, in the throbbing of her heart and all her arteries heading south.

Distracting her with kisses, Byrne eased her sweater up, freeing her breasts, warm now in his hands. She didn't fight him.

"Amy?" he said, and she read his mind. She smiled.

Slowly Byrne unbuttoned his vest and his dress shirt. He disposed of his tie. Then he pressed her eager, pointed breasts against his warm chest, just as he'd done at their first encounter.

They spoke no more. She looped her arms about his shoulders to show her cooperation in this reenactment of that lifesaving intimacy which neither had been in a mood to appreciate a week ago.

Both of them groaned from deep inside, tightening their embrace.

"Byrne, thank you for saving my life," she whispered.

"It was my pleasure," he responded with a grin.

As his left hand rubbed her shoulder, his right hand slowly strayed lower and lower until it cupped her breast. He squeezed it gently, and with the tip of his finger he traced her nipple, shooting fiery hot sensations to the core of her femininity.

Amy shivered and kissed him hungrily, wondering where this would end.

"When do you leave?" she managed to ask him.

"In a few days," he said. "I have no more time off, but I'll get up here every chance I can."

"Good," she said, waiting for his next statement.

Reading her thoughts, he added, "And not just to check on my niece either; you know that."

"Now I do," she said. So her feelings for him were already reciprocated.

"You know, you've changed, Amy," he said, resting his forehead against hers.

"In what way?"

"The last time I held you like this, I actually thought I was holding an ice maiden in my arms."

She started to giggle. "I was *that* cold?"

"I prefer you this way," he said. "In fact, you are one very warm lady."

At that exact moment Abercrombie let out a plaintive whine.

"Oh, no!" groaned Amy.

"What's the matter with him?" asked Byrne. "Why is he sticking his head through that little flap in your front door?"

"That's Cornflake's cat door. He can't squeeze through it, but that's how he tells me he has to go out."

"Really essential, uh?" Byrne said with a groan.

"Yes, really essential. I have all those big houseplants sitting around on the floor, and if I don't let him out pronto, he'll—"

"Don't tell me, I can guess," Byrne said, grinning. He released her to hop off his lap. Pulling her sweater down, she hurried to let Abercrombie out into the night.

When she faced Byrne Cooper again, Amy decided this interruption had been for the best. She had to slow things down.

"I have to get up at seven, Byrne. It's well past midnight."

"Caution rears its head?" he said. "Well, it's only our third date, I suppose." His face was momentarily glum, and then his eyes resumed their sparkle. He was man enough not to be offended—manly and considerate. He buttoned his shirt, got up off the couch, bent, and clasped her head between his warm hands. He rubbed noses with her in an Eskimo kiss.

"You're a good woman, Amy—smart, brave, beautiful, resourceful, and charming."

"I sound like a Girl Scout, some female Eagle Scout, studded with badges."

"I'd like to see you out of your clothes again," he mused, "wearing only your merit badges—the fewer, the better."

## CHAPTER TEN

The next few times they saw each other, Amy and Byrne did a lot of talking. Without actually saying it, both were aiming to get to know each other better before exploring further the sensual electricity that crackled between them. When Byrne ran out of taped talk shows, he returned to the radio station in Charlotte. It was obvious that he was reluctant to depart before Ronnie woke up and wasn't happy to be leaving Amy.

Half of April was over. The students at the academy where Amy worked had spring fever and lay about on the lawns, soaking up the thin sunshine. Like Cecelia several years before, many of the current crop of girls hung around the switchboard to tell Amy about their love problems.

Amy was invited nightly to the Coopers' for supper, and before or after eating with them, she visited the hospital to look in on Ronnie. Her cat and collie resented this change in her life-style, and she apologized for neglecting them. They were no longer her only family members.

Each evening between seven and nine, if she wasn't in her car, she slipped into a back bedroom of the Cooper house to tune in to the Charlotte station. She couldn't bear to miss the cadenced baritone of the man she was beginning to love.

"Tonight we'll be discussing emergencies," he said one evening as she drove home, and Amy knew he couldn't wait around for the naked mystery woman to reveal her true identity before discussing drowning victims on his show.

"Great strides have been made in rescue techniques," he began. "Remember the old diagrams showing a person lying facedown, being resuscitated by someone straddling him? How ineffective we now realize that is. Now we use mouth-to-mouth resuscitation."

Amy knew Byrne was good at that as well, if it was called kissing.

"There's even controversy," Byrne's voice continued, "over treating snakebites by cutting an X over the bite and sucking out the poison. Tonight experts will discuss new assumptions about lifesaving—right after this word from our sponsor."

The sponsor's "word," of course, bored Amy for three minutes before Byrne came back on. Turning up the volume, she cocked her head to hear better and squinted at oncoming headlights.

"How many people die every year because we don't know how to save them?" he asked.

Amy was a little disappointed at how briefly he covered cold-water drowning and at how little emotion he showed. She heard in his tone his disappointment that he couldn't make the topic fascinating, get some "angle" to hook audience interest.

When he invited listeners to call in, however, things livened up. "Mr. Cooper," said the first caller, a nasal-voiced woman, "was it you who was quoted in that newspaper article about saving a woman who dived into a pond to save a kid without clothes on?"

"Let's get that straight," he said, his voice a trifle strained. "Yes, I was on the scene when my niece was pulled from a pond in North Carolina back in March. The rescuer did not disrobe before she went into the water. Her clothes had to come off afterward so she could be treated for hypothermia. I just described the best treatment—body heat."

"Well," the woman said huffily, "that's not the impression *I* got from what you said about her."

Byrne's voice grew low and silky, almost a growl. "I'm not at all happy about being grossly misquoted and having a less than modest photo published of a very gallant young woman."

"She is still missing, isn't that so?"

Amy almost hit the car ahead of her.

"The rescuer never came forward to identify herself; that is correct. Thank you for sharing your thoughts with us tonight. Line two?" he said.

Technically he was correct, since she had run off and had never come forward to take any credit.

How widely was Byrne's show broadcast? Did his listeners live in the dark Appalachian Mountains the snowcaps of which were melting into bubbling cascades? Could his voice be heard across the Piedmont and the coastal plain to the Atlantic, where marsh birds waded and sand-dune grasses blew—all the way northeast to stormy Hatteras?

Amy kept her mind off Byrne Cooper by hanging out at the hospital, hanging over Ronnie Sue Cooper as the child came first out of her long barbiturate coma and then out of the natural coma, which had lasted two endless weeks so far. How would Sheila and the growing new baby survive many more weeks of running back and forth to the hospital? Would the Coopers' landscaping business fail?

Fortunately the two grandmothers and grandfathers were still there, and Sheila's blond brothers came down from High Point and Knoxville again. *Amazing,* thought Amy, *how families pitch in and help one another. I thought that sort of thing went out with the horse and buggy, along with community barn raisings.* So much of life she'd been totally unaware of, so much love she'd missed.

Ronnie Sue finally decided she'd missed enough of her fourth year of life, and Amy was there to witness the child's awakening. On the last day of April, in the evening when Amy was sitting by Ronnie Sue's bed, the child suddenly opened her eyes wide and stared. She not only stared but talked for the first time since her brush with death.

"Who are you?" she demanded.

"I've been reading to you a lot," Amy said, shivering with surprise. "When you fell in the water, I was there."

She kept talking to Ronnie, explaining what had happened, nodding responsively, and squeezing the little girl's hand. Amy pushed the call button, not daring to take her eyes off the child.

"It was cold," Amy said.

Sheila was just outside with her father-in-law. Seeing the light flash, they rushed into the room.

"Listen to this!" Amy excitedly said.

"I was cold," Ronnie said. "I want Pooh Bear."

Sheila couldn't move or speak. Tears sprang to her eyes.

"You shall have your bear," Ronnie's grandpa assured her. "Do you know who I am?"

"Gramps," she said. "Where've you been?"

"Right here," he said, gently taking her tiny hand. "We've all of us practically moved into the hospital to be with you, sweetheart."

"Hos-hospital?"

"This is a hospital," whispered Sheila. "They're making you well, darling."

Amy pulled Sheila closer, both of them teary-eyed as they watched the white-haired man bending over the child in the high bed. Ronnie finally focused on Sheila.

"Mommy!" she shrilled, and put out her arms. Sheila held and rocked her, murmuring endearments.

"Why are you crying, Mommy?"

"Because you woke up and I'm so happy."

"I got cold," she said determinedly, "in the dark."

"You sure did. But you're all warmed up now," said Amy.

The Coopers didn't get to take Ronnie Sue home for another two weeks. She graduated from intensive care to pediatrics, into a toy-crowded, love- and sunshine-filled room. She learned to walk again among small friends like her roommates with tonsillectomies and broken bones.

Amy loved to lift the little blond girl out of bed and lead her down the hall by the hand to the nearby solarium or to wheel her in a chair to physical therapy.

At night the events at Mackay's Pond rushed back to haunt Amy. Her nightmares now included scenes in which she waded a few inches to the left or right and therefore missed locating Ronnie underwater. It would have been nice to have someone in bed to hold her and ease her return to reality, but Byrne was off to New York and Philadelphia and couldn't be there.

Ronnie had lost weight, but now she was eating voraciously and gaining it back. When Ronnie's grandparents had to return home, and Sheila and Mike cut back a little on their heavy visiting schedule, Amy increased the length of her visits at the hospital. She read to Amy and played board games that the doctors had prescribed to exercise slowed reasoning abilities and to restore manual dexterity.

Unexpectedly the doctors moved Ronnie's release date up to May 23, a week earlier than planned.

Amy didn't expect the media to hear about it, but someone had tipped them off. Video cameramen and reporters from WHKP, WHVL, and WKIT arrived, and a reporter from the *Times-News*.

They'd been out of the news for two months. No onc besides the family seemed to have learned who the mystery rescuer was—a fact which pleased and amazed Amy. Even little Billy had kept the secret. Nurses and doctors were led to believe that the frequent visitor named Amy Barrett was Byrne Cooper's girl friend, maybe his fiancée, and therefore Ronnie's future aunt.

Amy stayed out of camera range as Mike and Sheila wheeled Ronnie down the hall toward the elevators. She didn't need a wheelchair any longer, but she loved the ride, blissfully smiling for the cameras. At the entrance to the hospital the Coopers gave an interview.

"We're so grateful to the wonderful staff of the medical center, who've loved our daughter like their own," said Mike. Sheila added her heartfelt thanks.

Amy guessed how difficult it was for them to leave her completely out of the spotlight—let her be a woman in the shadows, on the fringe of the family, nothing more. Fortunately Ronnie stole the show. Dimpling, playing Shirley Temple, when Ronnie was asked what she wanted to do first when she got home, she said, "Ride a pony!"

"But not go swimming!" one reporter remarked. Ronnie sent him a disgusted look that Amy relished. The only sad note was Byrne's absence. In his last phone call he'd said he had to go to Atlanta to interview the mayor.

However, when the Coopers' car, with Amy's following along behind, reached Orchard Lane, Byrne was getting out of his Lincoln parked at the curb.

"I heard on my car radio about Ronnie's release. I'm detouring on my way back to Charlotte," he shouted as Mike passed his car and swung up into the driveway.

Amy's eyes danced with happy anticipation as she watched Byrne unwind his big body from the Lincoln. She wasn't jealous when all his attention momentarily was directed at Ronnie; her turn would come. To see his face light up as he cuddled the little girl to his heart was as sweet to savor as a kiss.

After he'd held Ronnie Sue, studying her as closely as a father might examine his brand-new infant, Byrne handed her back to Sheila and turned to Amy. Face glowing, right there on the sidewalk he embraced and kissed her. She kissed him eagerly in return. When they came up for air, he gasped, "I hope the press at last gave you credit for the rescue."

"Nope, I've kept my secret," she said smugly, glad that no reporters had followed them home.

"That's unfair!" he retorted. "It's not fair to you."

Amy despaired of shutting Byrne up, but the best way to try was to cover his mouth with kisses.

On their way up the walk to the house Ronnie Sue offered a diversion. "Mommy's fat," she said.

"She's gonna have a baby," Billy informed his sister.

They all sat down to a late lunch prepared by Byrne's grandmother, who'd insisted on staying to "keep house." "What else have I got to do?" she'd snapped. "Those kids of mine—Byrne and Mike's parents—are so staid and boring."

Ronnie was wedged into her old high chair at the table because she wasn't completely steady yet, but she ate everything the rest of them ate. Nothing was wrong with her digestion, only with a few minor nerve pathways, which were gradually returning to good working order. Billy made no secret of appointing himself her guardian, watching every spoonful she maneuvered to her mouth and after lunch leading her out into the fenced yard. "Not near the gate," he told his parents solemnly.

"Ronnie's lucky to have you to watch over her," Byrne said as the small boy sat his sister down in the sandbox, and then he added, turning to Amy, "I've got to head for Charlotte soon. I can stay for only an hour more. I'm doing a show tonight."

## CHAPTER ELEVEN

Amy suggested that they leave Mom, Dad, the two kids, and grandma to get reacquainted. After hugs all around, she and Byrne strolled out to their cars.

"I've got to do the radio show tonight, and then tomorrow night there's a dinner-dance I have to emcee," he told her. "It's a fund raiser I got roped into for a political candidate—a friend of a friend. It may be dull, but, Amy, I want you there with me."

"You do? That's sweet of you, but—"

"Drive back to Charlotte with me, Amy. I have to be at the studio by seven for my show. You don't want to drive all the way there tomorrow in your old car."

"I could take the bus."

"Don't be silly. I'll follow you to your place, and you can grab some clothes and come with me."

"This may sound like a cliché, Byrne, but I have nothing to wear, not to a dinner-dance. I also have to feed my animals, shower, and do my hair." She released the strand of hair she'd been critically examining. It fell back on the collar of the yellow denim jump suit she'd been wearing when Mike called about Ronnie's leaving the hospital. This outfit was the one that little Billy labeled Amy's clown costume.

"C'mon. You look darling," he said, both his hands

ruffling her straight, fair hair as he studied her with such warmth that her knees wobbled. "You've got natural beauty; you don't need much time to primp. I'll bet I can find something in your closet that'll be perfect for tomorrow night."

She was relieved that he didn't suggest buying her some snazzy getup. She'd have to make do; she couldn't possibly afford any new clothes this month. The question she wanted to ask was why Byrne didn't have a date already for Saturday night. Charlotte was a big city, and this bash must have been arranged months in advance. If only she had two or three days to prepare, not just an hour or two!

Deep in the woods at her cabin, Byrne opened Amy's car door for her, saying, "You run and get ready, and I'll feed the furburgers."

He actually remembered her nickname for the animals! Amy stood on tiptoe to give him an affectionate kiss. A jaunt to the big city would indeed ease her withdrawal pangs. Now that Ronnie was out of the hospital, her new godmother wouldn't be so badly needed. The excitement that kept Amy's boredom at bay during her sedentary job was coming to an end, and rafting didn't begin for weeks yet.

Amy popped into the shower while Byrne fed the furburgers, dutifully adding brewer's yeast and leftovers to the cat food and collie food. Her friend Ellen, who also worked at the Academy switchboard, could feed them during her absence.

When she came out of the shower wearing one towel around her and one around her hair, Byrne was leaning into her closet, flipping through her clothes.

"Hey! What're you doing in there?" Amy demanded, almost dropping the towel that half covered her breasts.

"Hey, yourself!" He turned around to look at her. "Now, that's a cute outfit. I vote for that one. The papers will say, 'At the dinner-dance Amy Barrett was striking in sapphire terry cloth, by Cannon, her coiffure capped by a damp pink turban—' "

"You're a nut!" she said, ducking away from his reaching hands.

"I've seen Amy—and held her, too, as she might recall—when she was wearing a lot less than a towel."

"I recall. I certainly do recall!" she said, jerking her hips from side to side in a sort of hula to prevent his grabbing one end of the towel. "Be serious, Byrne! What do you suggest I wear tomorrow night?"

"What's this?" he asked, almost out of sight in her closet. She crowded in behind him, at the risk of losing her costume by Cannon. He pulled out a lacy cream-colored jacket crocheted in the Philippines. "Very nice," he said.

"I'd need something to wear under that, Byrne; it's a peekaboo weave."

"How about this?" He found the little black silk dress that her mother had given her years ago. She'd never had a funeral to wear it to.

Amy cocked her head to one side. "Not a bad combination. I'd never thought of putting those two together."

"May I help you dress?" he said, checking his watch as persuasion.

"Nope," she said, hunting for her lacy black slip and bra—other gifts from her mother. She herself had

106

bought some sexy summer sandals, which would go with the bell-sleeved crocheted jacket.

"We have to be on the road pretty quick—have to grab a bite on the way. Can your hair dry in the car?"

That's when Amy made her mistake. Reaching up to unwrap the towel from her hair, she neglected to keep at least one elbow tight against her ribs. The blue terry-cloth sarong began to slide.

Byrne, his mouth open to say something else, watched the towel drop down to the rug. His gaze flashed back up to the breasts Amy was trying to cover with the pink towel she'd pulled off her head.

"Oh, my sweet lovely!" he exclaimed, flinging an arm around her and sliding a hand under her bare knees. He scooped her up as easily as if she were Ronnie Sue Cooper. Distracted by the kisses across her temple and his murmurs of heartfelt admiration, she didn't resist as he laid her down on her bed and knelt over her. "I love you, Amy," he said. "I'm not going to Charlotte tonight."

"Your radio show! You can't miss being on the radio!"

"I'll make do," he said. "I've been stranded out of town before—once in a snowstorm. Call this a love-storm."

He reclined on the bed beside her, beginning an unbearably slow stroking of Amy's damply glowing, scented flesh. From the point of her chin to the dip of her navel, from hipbone across to hipbone, the fingers of his left hand lightly touched her, while his gaze locked on hers, and her arms lay limply beside her.

She'd waited too long for this. Resistance was out of the question. When she could command her hands to move, her fingers fluttered up to the buttons of his shirt, the knot of his tie. Without a word, she helped him undress, noting that his state of excitement matched hers.

"Amy, I'm falling in love with you," he murmured, no longer thinking about a fast trip to the city. Amy spent only a few more minutes wondering what his millions of listeners would think had happened to their radio guru. Then she invited and accepted the best reward she could imagine for having rescued Ronnie Sue: being skillfully, thoroughly, unhurriedly loved by Byrne Cooper.

"I'm going to find and taste all of last summer's freckles," he vowed.

Amy watched the squares of sunlight glide up the dark paneled walls, as he turned her to this side and that, honoring every freckle across her cheeks and her shoulders with a kiss, and then giving equal treatment to the deep dimples above her bottom, the soft back sides of her knees, and the arches of her feet. He caressed her with his lips and fingers, evoking hot, fluttery sensations that left her involuntarily gasping.

Amy finally summoned enough strength to pull herself up on her elbow and lean over him, placing kisses all across his wide chest, drawing her fingertips through the black hair of his chest and downward. His head hung half off the edge of the mattress, and his eyes were almost closed as he hissed, "Yes, yes, darling."

What joy to discover what pleased him most and then to slide down beside him again to receive pleasure in turn. They took their time as if nothing but them existed on earth. She deserved this, Amy knew, and so did he. Neither was taking advantage of the other, neither was selfish; both were in ecstasy.

Each of them gave joy and received it. Finally she invited Byrne to cover her with his body. On her soft bed, now striped with sunset pink and gold, she drew him into herself with a gasp and locked her arms about him as if she'd never let go. His lips on hers, his hands molding her hips, his tenderness unstinting, Byrne extended their joy, let it wax and wane until the sunset faded from the wall and their rumpled bedclothes. Their ultimate joy they drew out long and lingeringly, clinging to it, to each other, until Amy's eyes filled with tears, and she glimpsed the hint of tears in his eyes as well.

"I love you," he said huskily.

Amy looked up at him, unable to utter a word, but for the first time she knew for certain that he told the truth. He felt love, not just gratitude.

## CHAPTER TWELVE

When Amy awoke, she sat up in bed beside him, crying, "Byrne! What about your radio show?"

He squinted at his watch. "Oops! Six fifty-five. Good timing, darling. Where's your phone?"

"My phone? In the living room. Gee, it's chilly; I'll start a fire."

She lit the junk mail stuffed into her small cast-iron wood stove and opened its doors to display the flames. Byrne, dialing the telephone, settled down on the rug in front of her four-legged iron hearth.

Before Amy could again ask if he wasn't being irresponsible, if he'd get in Dutch with his station manager, she heard the melodious baritone say those so familiar words "Good evening. This is *Conversations with Cooper.*"

He was talking right into her telephone, not into a mike!

"It's Friday night," he said, "and the topic this evening is love."

Standing over him with an armful of logs from her woodpile, Amy gaped. On the telephone? He was on the air via telephone?

"... these words from our sponsor," he said,

waited for a moment, and then added, "Jim, just patch in the calls."

"What does that mean?" Amy whispered when she realized he was temporarily inaudible to his listeners.

Quickly he explained, "Our engineer down at the studio in Charlotte is mixing it through the board, plugging me in the way he'll patch in the calls. It's like a four-way telephone conference call: line one for me, and lines two, three, and four for the folks who'll call in."

She didn't get a chance to comment on his provocative topic for the evening before he was on the air again. He said, "By 'love,' I specifically mean keeping love alive, keeping the excitement in your relationship, in your marriage. We have no guest expert tonight; I want to hear from all of you. Three lines are open for your calls; dial 555-6060. Give us a call, and let's get this discussion under way."

Marveling, Amy fed the fire as quietly as she could and set the teapot on top of the wood stove to heat. When Abercrombie strolled over to stand in front of Byrne, wagging his plumed tail, Amy kneed the collie away from the busy talk-show host. She mouthed the question "Are you comfortable?"

Byrne gave her a big smile and a thumbs-up sign. Then he pointed at her radio. Amy understood. Crossing the room, she switched the radio on softly. Now she could listen to him both in person and—with a one-beat delay—over the radio. She could hear the callers and the commercials without sticking her ear next to Byrne's at the telephone receiver.

"Byrne, I've tried just about everything," a woman was saying, "trips for the two of us away from home,

111

dinner by candlelight, wine, flowers; none of it works."

"Let's clarify the situation," Byrne said in his resonant, confident voice. "Is it you or your husband who can't get inspired by these romantic settings?"

"It's me," she said. "He's fine. He can make love at any hour, any place, even outside in a rainstorm, I'd bet. I'm just so tired after work—"

"How old are you if I may ask?"

"I'm forty-three."

"Umm-hmm," Byrne said, shooting a look of perplexity at Amy. "How's your health, your stamina? Do you get a good diet and plenty of exercise?"

"I'm just a little overweight, and after sitting at an office desk all day long, I just can't bear to exercise. I'm always worn-out."

Amy snatched up the pad by the telephone and scribbled, "Walk or jog before work—gives more energy all day."

Byrne smiled gratefully. "It sounds as if your problem is not enough exercise. If you take a brisk walk or jog a little in the morning before work, you'll have more energy all day. This is advice from an expert on the subject. You realize that if you were to lie in bed all day, you wouldn't get stronger; you'd get weaker. Same principle. If you tone your body, you'll probably enjoy the indoor sport of love more as well."

"I never thought of that," she exclaimed. "I thought I was saving my strength for my husband. You think I'd better exercise, like join an aerobics class?"

Amy nodded vigorously.

"That would be even better," Byrne said. "It would

also increase your physical attractiveness and self-esteem."

When the water boiled, Amy made Byrne coffee. She settled down beside him, and during commercials they discussed his callers' problems. Amy had never had more fun than this. To be broadcasting from her own hideaway satisfied her needs for both privacy and interaction with other people.

The rug wasn't soft enough, though. After half an hour of sitting Amy went into the bedroom and dragged from under the bedsheet the sheepskin mattress pad her mother had given her. The resemblance between it and a fleece-lined coat was not lost on Amy or on Byrne either.

He shared a smile with her as she eased the fleece under them and around them and added more throw pillows to make a fleecy nest down on the rug, up against the sofa.

At the next commercial break he sighed and said, "You're spoiling me rotten, Amy. How can I ever again stand to broadcast from a cramped studio, all alone, pushing buttons?"

"You'll soon be a TV star," she reminded him.

Byrne told the next caller who was bored with sex to install an open-hearth wood stove. "Try making love on a sheepskin in front of the fire," he suggested.

Excited again by anticipation, Amy had to bury her face against Byrne's chest to keep her giggles from being broadcast to half the Carolinas.

Drinking coffee, grabbing bites of raisin cake, fielding calls, Byrne at the next break whispered to Amy, "You've got a problem, you speak on the phone as a caller."

113

"No problem!" she mouthed in reply.

"Then offer advice," he said.

Curled up in the crook of his arm, gazing at the fire, Amy waited through the first hour, entranced with the byplay among troubled or helpful callers whose voices issued from her radio and the wise, unruffled host who sat in her house a hundred miles from Charlotte. When a middle-aged homemaker came up with an unusual problem, Amy finally decided to speak up.

The woman and her husband lived out in the country; both were self-employed at home. "I go to town only once a week," the wife said. "I'm so wrapped up in my painting that I've gotten sick and tired of the time required to dress up, but wearing a bathrobe all day is a turnoff to my husband. What'll I do to please both of us?"

Amy motioned for the telephone.

"Line Two, you're on the air," said Byrne, and handed her the receiver.

"My mom had that problem," Amy blurted out, without bothering to say hello. "She invented a couple of offbeat costumes to wear around the house. She still has great legs, so she wears colorful thigh-length smocks over tights. Or she'll wear India cotton caftans. How about a set of jump suits? Pick yourself a sort of uniform but a cute, appealing one."

"No more chenille bathrobes or cotton housedresses then?" the caller said musingly. "I think that's a great idea."

Amy was grinning from ear to ear when she handed the telephone back to Byrne. She merrily fed the fire and fed Byrne while they communicated by facial expressions and gestures. She was delighted with hilarious calls about jealous pets and vibrators; she was sobered by sadder ones concerning illnesses and widowhood.

The only time Byrne showed his temper was when a woman asked why all his talk shows involved sex, "that totally foul and disgusting topic."

"I have the figures right here, ma'am," he said. "No more than thirty percent of my shows concern love and sex, and I keep it that low with difficulty. People need help, and frankly I suspect that you do, too—for instance, from a trained psychiatrist."

That caller put no damper on Byrne and Amy, who, after he had signed off for the evening, lay back, sighing, on the sheepskin and again made love. Theirs was a totally enriching activity made up of slow caresses and tender sharing.

Byrne slept with Amy that night, atop the sheepskin pad between sunshine-scented sheets. Her cat, Cornflake, walked across Byrne at 3:00 A.M. to settle down in a narrow space between him and Amy until she was gingerly removed by a large, hairy hand.

At noon the next day they took Abercrombie for a stroll along the river, snacked on cheese and fruit, and then Amy got herself all dolled up for the dinner-dance and eased herself into his Lincoln.

"By the way, your mom sounds like a neat person, Amy," he remarked as he drove out of Hendersonville. "I can just see her in those caftans and tights—a real Californian, huh? I'd sure like to meet her."

Wordless, Amy pointed out the window at one of the red barns and farmhouses she especially liked, adroitly changing the subject.

115

"You've met and charmed everyone in my family," he said before letting the subject drop.

They'd spent such a leisurely day at her hideaway that Byrne had to rush to his condo and leap into his clothes while Amy poked around in his kitchen and examined his curios and his houseplants.

He emerged looking smashing in a trim black tuxedo.

"I didn't know it was going to be *that* formal!" Amy gasped.

"I didn't dare tell you, my dear," he said. "But you're in black, too. You look gorgeous, by the way, so keep that little chin up."

"Going out with a guy in a tux!" she said. "That certainly takes me back to my unlamented youth, Byrne Cooper."

A tune started playing in her mind. It was not one of her mother's ballads, not a song from high school days when boys in tuxes squired her to dances. It was a song from *A Chorus Line:* the song describing the things one does for love.

## CHAPTER THIRTEEN

That evening Amy felt like pulling another disappearing act. She'd guessed correctly. The metropolitan social whirl certainly wasn't for her. Sitting on the dais beside Byrne in the elegant ballroom, dining on prime rib, she was constantly ogled. Was she being hypersensitive? No. People at the tables below them seemed to make a show of glancing up at her and Byrne and then whispering to each other behind their hands.

After the dull speeches which followed Byrne's interesting brief talk on the qualities of a true leader, champagne started flowing. For many guests, tact was washed away. Tipsy society women boldly cuddled up to Byrne while archly eyeing Amy. Watching him trying to be minimally polite was painful, and Amy hesitated to join in the conversations that sounded interesting. She didn't want to try to explain who she was and how she'd met Byrne Cooper.

Amid the glitter and glitz roamed portly, flushed men in tuxes who patted Amy on the arm—and later in the evening—on the bottom. Some seemed pleasant and intelligent, but then wives appeared and unceremoniously jerked them away. They glared at Amy as if she were the notorious Evelina Sloan herself. How silly, when she was interested in only one man at the party—the most attractive, articulate man there. Byrne's having "Eligible Bachelor" written all over him made him a magnet for women, Amy told herself. She mustn't feel jealous or paranoid, but hearing in loud whispers, "He's dating the gal in the bargain basement outfit?" and "Where'd he dig *her* up?" made her contemplate flight—or murder.

Byrne had enough sense not to ask, "Having a good time?" He danced the first two dances with her, and then he dutifully mingled with the other guests, shaking hundreds of hands. She chose to sit with a couple of sweet elderly ladies, putting a potted fern between her and the men she turned down as dance partners.

It didn't help that the orchestra played two of her mother's most popular songs, the vocalist doing an inferior job on the lyrics.

Byrne made many circuits past her chair to check on her. Once he bent and whispered, "These are not my best buddies. I don't even vote the way most of them do."

On their way home he listed the charities for which he preferred to be emcee or fund-raising chairman: the Heart Association, the Easter Seal Society, Little League, and the American Cancer Society.

"I certainly picked the wrong party to take you to," Byrne said apologetically, his sorrow making Amy bite her tongue to remain silent. Tonight she'd felt like a kid again, dragged to a noisy, drunken party with Mom or lying awake in bed as the riot went on downstairs in their house, afraid a guest or two might come wandering upstairs.

"Remember, I'm a country girl," she said. "Your life and mine are totally different." She couldn't look at him; she didn't add, *And they'll remain that way—different and separate.* In effect, she'd just said good-bye.

"I don't agree," Byrne told her, driving into the parking garage beneath his condo. "Tonight you saw the very worst I have to go through. Some of those women have come on to me; they'd give anyone I dated a hard time, and you were a total novelty."

"Who'd you say I was, Byrne?"

He groaned out a sigh. "That was tough; everyone asked. If I'd admitted you were from Hendersonville, some would surely remember the mystery woman featured in that tabloid. I had to say you lived in Charlotte, but I avoided saying anything else."

"I knew I'd be completely out of place among rich people interested in politics. I'll bet no one wore shoes that cost less than my whole outfit did."

"That's silly. You were a knockout, Amy! Guys were clustering around you so eagerly I wasn't sure whether you wanted to be rescued or not."

"I wanted to be rescued," she said, "but I saw you had your own hands full. Look, I don't blame you, Byrne. We just revolve in different orbits. Your sister-in-law, Sheila, probably wouldn't have enjoyed tonight either."

"You're absolutely right. Sheila wouldn't go near a cocktail party—on moral principles. They might send a check, but they'd never attend a benefit featuring liquor and dancing."

"Not even dancing? Boy, I'd better be on my best behavior at their house!"

"Look, honey," he said, twisting in his seat to cup her face between his big warm hands, "there is nothing on earth that could lessen the loving gratitude they feel—that all of us feel for you."

She wished she could believe him.

Amy rode a Greyhound bus home to Hendersonville on Sunday afternoon, sorry to be leaving Byrne behind in Charlotte but relieved to see the Blue Ridge and the Smokies rising azure and misty before her. She was going home to the woods, to the hills, to the river. Realizing how impossible their situation was, she'd refused to continue the marvelous physical union that was going to be agony to relinquish.

Byrne's tenderness and his regret and penitence were exemplified by the snack he cooked for her at 2:00 A.M. It made her decision to close out their relationship just that much harder.

"I really would prefer to go rafting on your river," he said, "or to lie in the summer grass reading a good book, but my job requires socializing with the public. They support my show, which, unless I'm fooling myself, does a lot of good."

"Yes, I think it does," she'd said, nursing her cup of Postum and her grilled cheese sandwich, trying not to look at him.

"You ought to hear the battles I have with the station manager over topics on my show. He wants to keep it light. I want to educate. Did you know I taught sociology in high school for a few years after I got my master's degree? I want to cover topics like the causes of child abuse and rape, like organized crime, pollution, nuclear energy, and nuclear war. To do so, I have to find an angle to make those topics fascinating— meaning shocking. I see myself as one of the Ralph

Naders of the airwaves, but tonight you must have seen me as a prostitute, cultivating a lot of people I wouldn't choose for friends."

"I truly felt sorry for you, Byrne; that was the main thing that bugged me. I know you well enough by now to recognize what you were going through, what you have to go through. Just count me out. I can't bear to watch."

"Did you grow up in a city or on a farm, Amy? I'd bet on the farm. You've never told me anything about your background except that your mom wears Indian caftans."

"It's not interesting," she'd told him. "My mother lives in California with her fifth husband. My dad was her first one. He's dead. They got married after I was born, and in those days that was plenty shocking. The other kids Mom had grew up with their fathers after the divorces."

He'd contemplated her soberly and sadly. "That's no way to grow up trusting people, is it? I could sense that from the first."

He'd tried to kiss her for comfort, but she'd twisted away, suppressing the urge to cling to him, to make love with him and forget their differences. That would've been stupid.

She'd slept Saturday night in Byrne's condo, but not in his bed. She refused to fall any further in love—fall and break her own heart and his as well.

Now, as the bus neared Hendersonville, she had the comfort of Mother Nature's beauty spread out before her. This season foliage came in dozens of shades of green. Time ran backward as the bus climbed; they left early summer and returned to spring. Green leaves

121

gave way to pale baby leaves. Deciduous trees gave way to pine, spruce, and fir, which climbed the highest mountains, dark and dramatic on the under slopes.

Her business partner, Irene, was in town now, and the rafting season would begin as soon as the school year ended at the academy and Amy was free. Irene would keep her busy recruiting rafters from summer camps in the area. They'd float calmly, then bounce excitingly through the rapids of the French Broad River all summer. She'd get over Byrne Cooper.

Amy, however, didn't miss one day of listening to Byrne on the radio. She even bought a pocket-size radio with a button she screwed into her ear. Subconsciously she began to sense hints of his awareness that she was tuned in—tuned in to him, but not in tune with him.

He asked callers to share their advice about what makes a happy marriage. "What keeps some people together who seem to be totally different?" he asked. "Is it that they give each other plenty of space and freedom to develop as individuals?"

"Yes, they'd do that," whispered Amy.

"My husband," said a woman who called in, "doesn't like me to ask, 'May I go visit my mother?' or 'May I buy a new dress?' "

"He forbids you to?" asked Byrne gruffly. Amy visualized his scowl.

"No! Not at all! It's the opposite!" she cried. "He doesn't like to hear me ask permission. He says that makes our relationship seem as if I'm a child and he's my daddy. 'I don't own you, Carol!' he says."

"I think I'd like your husband," Byrne said. "What do you say instead? 'Would you be inconvenienced if I went away for a week?' and 'Do you agree that I can afford a new dress this month?' "

The woman on the radio vehemently agreed. Byrne said, "God bless you, you lucky people."

Amy blinked rapidly as she knelt on the shore, inspecting the rubber rafts for leaks. She'd inflated them with a bicycle pump, and they gave off a pungent rubbery odor in the June sun. The light wasn't gone until Byrne's evening show was well under way. She could listen to him outdoors as well as inside, on the river as well as in her cabin. Listening to Byrne's show made her miss him. When he telephoned, as he did frequently, she tried to limit their conversation to Ronnie Sue and his family.

She took Abercrombie to visit Ronnie and Billy, and the lazy, big collie lounged luxuriously while the children took turns combing his fluff.

"He's the same color gold as your hair, Amy," said Sheila, still full of compliments, still wearing her heart in full view, throbbing with gratitude. "How do you keep him groomed so well?"

"I don't comb him more than once a month," Amy said. "He stands outside, and the wind does it; he's blow-styled."

Mike and Sheila grinned, gazing at her fondly. It was Mike who'd forced her to take home loaves of fresh baked bread and the first flowers from their garden. Amy didn't have flowers blooming yet, and the lawn around her cabin wasn't grass, but pine needles.

Byrne's peppery little grandmother, who was still at Orchard Lane, gave her even more. Apparently she had money. Ruby ordered Amy to drive her down to the nicest shop in Hendersonville, and once there, she threatened to fake a heart attack if Amy didn't cooperate. Amy had to try on a bunch of dresses, pants, and blouses and select several of each.

Suspended between incredulous amusement and consternation, Amy said, "Would you actually blackmail a person by pretending to be dying?"

"Of course I would! I'm not big enough or strong enough to get my way, but I'm rich enough, clever enough, and mean enough. Don't you doubt it." She sized up Amy. "What's your relationship to my grandson by now?"

"I think we're far too different to—to make anything of our friendship," Amy said, being as frank with Ruby Cooper as she'd been with Byrne.

"Different? I think you two are exactly alike. I'd like to see you married."

Amy gulped, unable to look into Ruby's shrewd face across the table as they were eating lunch.

"Byrnie's been single for far too long. He'll get stuck in his ways. Humph!" she said. "That talk show of his a couple of days ago was all about marriage, but no one said, 'Be sure to marry before your habits get set in concrete.' *I* say, 'Don't marry before twenty-one or after thirty-one.' He's going on thirty-five. I want to see him hooked and landed, and the way he looks at *you,* girl—"

"That's pure gratitude, you know that."

"It's not just gratitude, and I hope it's not too pure either. If he doesn't move fast, he's going to have you drowning yourself on that river. Rafting—fancy that! You already came close to dying; he had to save you. Don't you realize that was fate's way of throwing you two together?"

124

"Fate, huh?"

"My other grandson says it was God's doing; Mike's religious, but I call it fate. That covers more bases."

"I think you're great," said Amy, and moved around the table so she could hug the delicate-looking old woman in her flower-sprigged dress and little black straw hat. Ruby wore no caftans. She looked like a caricature of a sweet little old lady till she opened her mouth.

"So marry Byrnie, become my granddaughter," she commanded. "You could do worse."

Amy drove home thoughtfully, and as she draped her expensive new clothes over her couch and chairs to admire them, she began to realize something. One reason she treasured Byrne's great-grandma so much was that the woman reminded her of someone. She reminded Amy not only of her grandson, Byrne, who'd inherited her quick intelligence, verve, and zip, but also of—of her own mother, of the best in her own mother, minus the worst.

## CHAPTER FOURTEEN

The following week something happened to Amy that she couldn't have predicted and would have avoided if she'd had any warning.

Sheila didn't warn her, however. When Amy's phone rang right after supper, the tone of Sheila Cooper's voice worried Amy.

"What's wrong, Sheila?" she asked. "You sound odd. Is anything the matter with Ronnie? Or with Grandma Ruby?"

"Nope, Grandma arrived home in Norfolk just fine, and Ronnie's still moving along right on schedule," she said. "Look, Amy, we need you. Can you come over tonight?"

"Well, sure . . ."

"It feels awful for me to be asking you a favor, considering what you've done for us, but—"

"Don't be silly; we're sisters," Amy interrupted. "I'm part of your family." In fact, being an adopted in-law to Byrne was the most she was going to allow herself to be.

"Okay, well, can you drive over right now? There are some people here I'd like you to meet. And, Amy," she added, "Mike doesn't know I've called you. Will you pretend you just dropped in—pretend to Mike and to these people as well?"

Slightly on edge by now, Amy asked, "Do these people know who I am, I mean, what I did?" Her mental antennae were picking up dread or guilt.

"No. Oh, no, they don't know you were the one who rescued Ronnie. We never tell people about that; it's up to you whether or not you keep your secret, Amy."

Relieved, Amy hung up the phone, turned off the propane flame under the teapot, and slung a sweater around her shoulders against the cool evening at twenty-two hundred feet above sea level.

She deserted her forest hideaway for Orchard Lane, where she found that the mysterious "people" visiting Sheila were a young married couple. Little Ronnie, dressed in her fuzzy pink sleep suit, sat perched on the dark-haired woman's lap beside a bespectacled man who was asking her to name each feature of her stuffed panda bear.

"Nose!" Ronnie squealed. "Eye! Another eye! Ear! Two ears, see?"

"Isn't she a doll?" Amy began, coming straight over to drop a kiss on the silken blond head and squeeze the little hand extended toward her.

Mike sprang up, obviously surprised at her arrival. Sheila continued the deception, saying with feigned surprise, "It's so sweet of you to stop by, Amy!" as Ronnie grabbed the panda by the leg and yelled, "Foot!"

"This is Jan Glouster," Sheila said breathlessly. "This is her husband, Dick. Jan, Dick, Amy Barrett is

127

a friend of ours. Amy, the Glousters lost their little boy two years ago."

So that was it! The anger that swelled in Amy promptly deflated like a balloon or a rubber raft, leaving her incapable of saying a word. She knew exactly what was coming.

"Their little boy wasn't as lucky as Ronnie," Sheila continued, turning expectantly toward the wan-faced woman, who perhaps wasn't near thirty, after all. She was prematurely aged.

"Yes, our Jason drowned," said Jan, looking up at Amy past Ronnie's golden head. "It was two years ago."

"Drowned in just a few inches of water in a ditch near our house," her husband explained, as if talking about it eased his pain.

Amy's pain didn't ease. It kept on growing. "Mmm," she said, "I'm awfully sorry to hear that."

Jan continued, "He was only twenty-one months old, and it happened in cold weather, the same as with Ronnie. We wonder if—"

Face averted, Mike sprang up and headed for the kitchen, mumbling, ". . . get more coffee."

"You mustn't blame yourselves," Sheila said. "You didn't know what to do. *I* didn't know anything either."

"But that woman who saved Ronnie knew," said Jan, making Amy's stomach rock like a cradle inside her and her feet and hands feel as if she'd stuck them in a freezer.

Sheila was trying not to look at Amy. She lifted Ronnie off Jan's knees, saying, "It's past her bedtime. Please excuse us for a sec."

128

Amy was left alone in the living room with the Glousters, staring them right in the face, mute. Dick Glouster resumed talking.

"We're from Decatur, Georgia," he explained. "When we saw the newspaper story about Ronnie, we just had to get up here to see her, see for ourselves."

"We're trying to gather data," said his wife.

People with a cause, Amy knew, seldom had time or energy to waste on small talk.

"We think the Coopers ought to write a book about Ronnie's survival," said the man. "Then they could go on television, go public so other parents will know what to do if, God forbid, they should find themselves in a similar situation. We're certainly not the only ones to lose a child from drowning."

Dick had his arm around his wife. "Jason's face was underwater for only about ten or twelve minutes," he murmured.

"Please," interrupted Amy, afraid she was going to be sick.

Jan tapped her husband's knee warningly. "Forgive us. It's all we've thought about since we heard about Ronnie. We often bore people and depress them; we can't seem to discuss anything else."

"No, we can't," said Dick, frowning at Amy over his rimless spectacles.

Amy wondered if his hair had started graying when his son died or when they realized the death might have been prevented.

When Sheila came back, her gaze darted from one face to another. Wired, she resumed chattering immediately. "I've explained to Dick and Jan how busy we are, trying to keep our business afloat, after those

129

months at the hospital . . . all the bills to be paid. We wouldn't know the first thing about writing a book."

"Your husband's brother was involved in the accident, and he's a radio star," said Dick. "He could get media attention."

"Byrne wants to spread the word," Sheila admitted, still avoiding more than a glance at Amy. "It's just that—"

"You still haven't found out who the rescuer was?" asked Jan.

Sheila fell silent. The sudden silence horrified Amy. She remembered her last argument over the phone with Byrne and how he'd said, "Where does shyness end and selfishness begin, Amy? Some people say extreme shyness is a symptom of egocentricity. You can't see others' needs because you're focused entirely upon yourself."

She hated his thinking of her like that, but she hadn't quite given in. This, however, was too much. The silence in the Coopers' living room formed a vacuum that was going to suck the truth right out of her.

Rather than run away again, rather than be selfish and egocentric, Amy unsealed her lips at last. "I was the one," she said in a soft monotone. "I pulled Ronnie out of the pond."

The Glousters swung around to her, their pale faces like twin radar dishes, their eyes magnified through the tears Amy couldn't blink away.

"You were the woman in the photo?" Jan whispered. "That was you?"

"Yes, without my clothes on. I realize I've been awfully selfish. Secrecy helped no one."

Sheila rushed across the room to Amy. "Oh, please

130

don't blame yourself! Don't apologize. You had the right—"

"The right to remain silent?" Amy said. She silenced Sheila with a lifted hand. "I deserve some blame. Byrne's been begging me to go public, to exploit that tabloid story—photo and all. All I can say," she rushed on, afraid the Glousters would start in on her, "is that if your son had died *after* Ronnie's experience rather than before, I'd feel like cutting my stupid throat!"

"Oh, Amy, don't say that!" cried Sheila. "We love you!"

"You'll do it, then?" Dick Glouster asked. "You'll go on TV? You'll explain how to prevent other deaths?"

Amy nodded, looking down at her hands. "I've never met people who'd lost a child . . . that way. I'm not a mother myself. Yes, I'll help, I promise."

Mike finally came back into the room, carrying a steaming carafe of coffee.

"Mike," said Sheila.

"You missed the change-of-heart scene." Amy sighed.

Amy refused to drink coffee. She wouldn't sleep for a week if she added caffeine to her consternation. The moment she got home, she placed a long-distance call to Charlotte, North Carolina, and a thrillingly familiar, beloved voice said, "I'll get back to you as soon as possible if you'll leave your name, number, and a message." He was prerecorded even at home.

Amy didn't hesitate. She said, "Byrne, I want you to go ahead and book me on radio or TV. Do it right away, Byrne. I've just seen the light."

131

She hadn't got an answer from Charlotte by dawn on Saturday, when she loaded up the two rubber rafts with rafting and camping equipment from her store-room, tied them together, and paddled down the river toward Pisgah. She and Irene operated their rafting business from a shack onshore, which they boarded up from October to June.

Ads they'd put in the paper and posted around town had attracted their first dozen rafters for a two-day trip. "No one under eight years old" was their rule in this region full of summer camps. Amy was especially glad about that rule nowadays when drowning kids obsessed her.

Irene's brother, Pete, was a rafting guide on the Gauley River up in West Virginia. Amy had traveled there to be trained before applying for certification in North Carolina. She'd learned to shoot Class IV and V rapids, terrifying roller coasters through which the rafts' incredible twisting, bucking, and tossing consti-tuted an insane defiance of gravity.

Amy had conquered gut-level terror and learned ab-solute respect for the river. She had also learned to give absolute obedience to the expert guides who told rafters when to paddle or bail as the flimsy rafts climbed six-foot walls of water and then dropped off rock ledges into holes, viciously jolting the soaked rafters. She'd often found herself staring at a raft's floor rising vertically before it flipped all of them out into the swirling maelstrom.

The French Broad was a totally different river. Amy adored shooting its gentler rapids. Class III rapids did require preparatory scouting, eddy to eddy, because

132

the flow varied with rainfall and snow melt. Amy and Irene picked routes to avoid holes and the treacherous backwash below drops. Even old people liked to go rafting with them.

When they could afford to purchase wet suits to rent to rafters, they could outfit groups earlier in the season. In June they just tried to keep everyone in life jackets . . . and in the rafts.

Saturday morning, while Irene drove downtown to pick up people, Amy got ready to collect the seventy-dollar fee that covered equipment, instruction, insurance, and four meals en route. She didn't even see the white car slide into the limited parking space they'd cleared between their outfitters' shack and the put-in spot.

"I didn't call; I came," he said.

Amy almost got whiplash jerking her head up from the money-box. There he stood in jeans and a green-and-red flannel shirt.

"Byrne!"

"You're starting a raft trip here this morning? That's what posters say all over town: 'Raft with Irene and Amy.' "

"I'll be so awfully busy," Amy said fretfully. "I won't have one minute to talk before we're afloat." She was trying not to remember his kisses, his touch, his taste, and his incredible skill at satisfying desires she hadn't known she still had.

"Count me in," he said, reaching for his wallet. "What is it? Two days and a night for only seventy dollars? A steal."

"But we're all booked up for this trip," she muttered in disappointment, devouring the sight of the big man, his brand-new tan making his black brows less threatening by contrast. He was dangling his sheepskin coat over one shoulder by a hooked finger, inadvertently reminding her of that evening in March—or was it inadvertent? Today's temperature might reach eighty, but he'd brought that coat along, the cozy cocoon from which she'd emerged damp and rumpled but able to try her wings—and fly away from him.

"Maybe someone will cancel," he said hopefully. "That happens, doesn't it? I'll wait around. We need to talk."

They certainly did need to talk. She could imagine how early he must have arisen to arrive here from Charlotte at eight in the morning.

"How about a kiss, Amy?"

Before she could reply, he backed her through the door into the outfitters' shack, dropped his coat over the only chair, and drew her into his arms.

Their kiss wasn't the kiss of a couple who were breaking up. Against her wind-chilled skin, his face felt as warm as the big, caressing hands that steadied her head. Warm lips caressed her lips, parted them, and she could think of nothing but conquest and surrender as his tongue sought hers and calmly took possession.

Squeezing her eyes tightly shut, Amy put both arms around him, gripping her own wrists Indian-style. She hugged him so tight that a slighter man might have grunted.

"Rafting really gives you muscles," he murmured into her ear, tickling it deliciously with his tongue. He nipped at locks of hair feathering across her temple. "Amy, I want you."

134

"You're glad I'll go public now?" she asked.

He straightened up, glaring down at her. "That is *not* the reason I'm kissing you, Amy, you little nut! Gratitude is not my motivation—not now and not back in March either. Can't you get that through your head? I happen to have fallen for you. Meeting the way we did just accelerated my feelings for you."

They shared another deep, ravenous kiss before Amy came up, sputtering. "Sheila lured me over to her place and exposed me to people whose child drowned . . ."

"Good ol' Sheila! We'll get right on it. I'm taping talk shows for TV next week. Come back to Charlotte with me Monday, and we'll get Ronnie and Sheila down, too, and a doctor or two—"

"You can arrange it that fast?" she asked.

"I'm not letting go now that I've got your cooperation, kid!"

Amy burrowed her face for a moment into the base of his neck, deep into his plaid flannel shirt with the bleach-scented white T-shirt beneath. She sighed. "It's pretty sudden."

What she didn't spout off about was that even while she was refusing to go on the air about Ronnie's case, she hadn't wasted her time. She'd spent many hours in the hospital library, digging through the literature on resuscitation. She'd also spoken with Ronnie's doctors in the ICU. She remembered enough of her college physiology course that medical terminology didn't throw her.

"Hmmm, Amy, your description sure fits!"

The amused voice belonged to Irene. Amy's partner hadn't had to identify Byrne from Amy's description alone either. Their embrace, arms locked around each other, announced who he was.

"Byrne Cooper, meet Irene Bienhomme," said Amy, enjoying Irene's expression as she assessed the tall, rugged radio personality. Amy knew he'd comment on their contrasting appearance; Irene was as small and dark as Amy was tall and fair.

"You're the rafting partner," Byrne said, sticking out his hand. "I've heard about the little mesomorph who can manage to outpaddle this deceptively delicate ectomorph here."

"Yep, he does have a way with words off the air as well as on," Irene confided in a stage whisper to Amy. "Yep," she said to Byrne, "I'd like to see some more meat on Amy's bones for insulation. By the end of the summers, though, she really starts busting out in muscles."

". . . rather than busting out in the bust!" Amy said kiddingly, accustomed to trading puns with Irene. "No, forget I said that! Guess what, Irene? Byrne wants to go rafting with us this weekend."

"Well"—Irene consulted her clipboard—"one customer named Kevin Fox, age ten, just withdrew from our party. Measles."

"Great," said Byrne. "Or would two ten-year-olds have to drop out to make room for me? I weigh one-ninety."

"That's okay," said Irene. "You can furnish a lot of power per pound. You ever been rafting before?"

"Never. A first time for everything." He cocked a brow at Amy.

"Okay," Amy said, stepping into the tiny office with a window making it resemble an old-fashioned movie show ticket booth. "Over here!" she called to the knot of people who'd disembarked from Irene's van and were uneasily contemplating the water. "Let's get this show on the river!"

# CHAPTER FIFTEEN

Before the dozen set out upon the river in the two rafts, Amy and Irene gave them a joint lecture. While both sexes from age eleven to age sixty struggled into bright orange life jackets, Irene stressed obedience.

"When either Amy or I give an order," she said, "you shall obey. You got that? The safety of the whole group depends on everyone's observing that law. We don't just drift through the rapids. Your guide steers, and when she says 'Now!' you paddle as hard as you can. If you're knocked overboard—on this river that's unlikely—float downstream feetfirst with your toes up out of the water. We'll come get you."

That sobered everyone. Sneaking a glance at Byrne's furrowed brow, Amy took over. "No alcoholic beverages are allowed in the rafts," she said. "We all have to be sharp-witted. Tents for tonight and the other gear will be waiting for us at the overnight campsite along with steaks and other yummies. Packed lunches are aboard the larger raft in that waterproof cooler. Any questions?"

After Irene had had another say, and both of them had answered questions from the first-timers and the worriers, Amy felt Byrne touch her shoulder.

"You done good," he whispered. "Now I've learned

you have a knack for public speaking. That's great news."

Amy didn't have to ask why. He must be planning her grand debut on TV.

"This seems quite an expedition to expedite," Byrne murmured to Amy as he helped a middle-aged woman into a raft. She had no doubt which raft Byrne would choose. Amy perched up on the stern with her long paddle serving as both oar and rudder. She paired Byrne in the center with another husky man and put two young boys in the stern, where she could watch them. The two women sat up front.

They got short paddles, which Amy demonstrated how to use—leaning out over the side of the raft and digging straight down into the water. They could paddle forward, backpaddle, or drift; she'd tell which ones to do what—and when.

"We can let the current carry us for the first couple of miles," Amy told her crew of six as she pushed the raft off from shore. "Now's the time to practice paddling and following instructions."

She took the lead so Irene could keep them in view. Irene and her brother and her fiancé had been rafting since childhood, making Amy by comparison a novice.

"Wouldn't this be fun for Ronnie and Billy?" Byrne said back over his shoulder.

Amy shuddered. She had no desire to see either of the Cooper kids near water ever again, though common sense told her both of them ought to get swimming lessons pronto.

The air had been cleaned by last night's rain. The river was translucent jade near shore, under the boughs of the basswoods and hemlocks, and golden in the sun, its current swift as it drained the still-snow-capped mountains. Everyone smiled, drawing in chestfuls of the June air, fragrant with rich, warming humus, flowing sap, and wild flowers.

No sweat. Steering was easy, and she was blessed with her crew, a pair of eager, polite preteen boys from one of the camps and the grandmothers up front who weren't inexperienced. Amy kept flicking her glance to the shiny black hair of Byrne Cooper, to his blessedly wide shoulders and strong back in the plaid flannel shirt. Her own lifesaver, oddly enough, today knew a lot less than she did about water and danger. In fact, she didn't even know if he could swim.

The first rapids, only Class II, had the little boys chattering to each other, gripping their paddles with white knuckles. The sensation of the rocks sliding under them as the raft buckled and bent visibly shocked them and Byrne as well. He glanced back at Amy, wide-eyed, as she shouted, "Paddle! Now!" The first drop was only a few inches, but her paddlers tilted inboard, away from the foaming suds of the white water, clustering together for safety. People accustomed to rowboats and inner tubes didn't realize what a raft can do to limbs and torso. They braced themselves as she yelled, "Left side, backpaddle! Now! Everyone paddle forward! Now!"

Jolt followed jolt! Even a bucking bronco would furnish a more stable seat than the soft-bottomed raft. It was amazing that few rafters were ever killed.

The first Class III rapids appeared ahead, and Amy glanced back at Irene's raft before steering for the best passage through. *"Now!"* she shouted, and got a flurry of paddling that taxed everyone's skills. Over the rush of water piling up among rocks into three-foot waves, she could hear everyone huffing and puffing.

Amy was grateful that Byrne was aboard. Even with no experience, he'd learned fast; he obeyed her instantly. When his paddle dug into the boiling waves, the raft responded nicely. Slam, slam, whoosh! and they'd shot it and come riding into calmer waters. Six faces swung toward her, eyes squinting, every face wearing a jewel of a grin.

At noon she slung a rope around a shoreline rock, mooring for lunch. Irene floated the cooler over on a tether with their half of the sandwiches, deviled eggs, apples, and soda pop.

The kids decided to take a dip before eating but scrambled back aboard rather quickly, out of the chilly water.

"I've never felt I earned a meal more," commented Byrne, leaning back luxuriously with his boots off and his bare feet in the water.

The two boys ate so fast that she put them to work bailing the sloshing bottom of the raft. They wanted reassurance. "We get steaks and homemade pie for supper, right?" they asked.

"Yes, as well as potatoes baked on hot coals, salad, and hot cocoa—and you'll have earned it."

Later in the day that's exactly what Amy and Irene grilled, baked, tossed, and brewed for their rafters while everyone helped set up the two big tents, one for the men, one for the women. They shook out sleeping bags and unrolled foam mats. The breeze was stiff enough to blow away paper plates before food weighted them down, but no mosquito could get aloft, and that was a blessing.

"I never realized how still and unmoving the solid earth can feel," Byrne marveled.

He joined in as the rafters relived every rapid they'd shot, gesticulating, their faces bronzed by the sun and the glow from the campfire as dusk deepened. Amy noticed that Byrne was letting everyone call him Ben. They hadn't caught his unusual first name and didn't recognize his face or voice. When he had his own show on TV, Amy realized, this luxury, the treat of mixing anonymously with people, would be denied him. Well, that was the life he'd chosen. It must have rewards greater than its obvious disadvantages.

"Butter? Sour cream?" Irene called, uncovering a plastic bowl of each under the noses of the hungry mob seated on tarps around the fire. Amy forked foil-wrapped potatoes out of the coals, keeping an eye on the steaks on the grill.

"How many for apple pie and how many for cherry?" was her final question after the coffee, beer, and cocoa had gone around.

A few of the sated rafters were now sprawled at full length on the tarpaulins. Three of the kids in the group were nearly asleep. Byrne stayed close beside Amy, sitting at right angles to her body, so she could lean back on his knees for support.

"Best decision I ever made," he commented, massaging the start-of-season soreness out of her shoulders. "I came up just to see you. I didn't expect to spend a wonderful day on the river."

"Two days almost," she corrected him. "We hit the takeout point about three tomorrow afternoon."

"Will you look at that?" he murmured in her ear.

The rising moon was shinnying up the far side of a

pine, making the whole tip glow, radiating silver beams.

"It's beautiful," Amy said.

"C'mon," he said, "you've worked awfully hard. Paper plates don't get washed; they get burned. Let's take a walk."

"Walk in the dark forest alone with you?" she asked jokingly. "That's not a very sensible thing for Li'l Red Ridinghood to do."

"Who's afraid of the Big Bad Wolf?" he retorted, struggling up off the tarp and helping her to her feet.

Amy certainly wasn't. She loved the big good wolf, who put his arm protectively around her waist. Irene glanced at them over her shoulder as she knelt, warming her hands at the fire. Almost imperceptibly she gave them a nod and a smile. How sad that Irene's fiancé, Dan, was studying down at N.C. State this summer, Amy thought. Irene's loneliness gave Amy a deeper appreciation of Byrne. How could she have been so dumb as to imagine she could give him up?

Byrne and Amy found a path that ran parallel to the river and followed it, stepping very carefully over rocky outcrops and eroded gaps. It was impossible to walk side by side.

"Here," he said, turning away from the river and hoisting her up a cliff to a flat, grassy-topped prow of land that offered a view of the moonlit river. There was still enough wind to discourage mosquitoes.

He spread his heavy coat, woolly side up, on the grass and, reclining upon it, pulled her down beside him, into his arms.

"I love you, Amy," he said.

"Don't say that."

143

"How about 'I am so proud of you'?"

"Proud of what?"

He lay with his lips to her forehead, moving his hands slowly up under her sweater. The dewy grass smelled as sweet as flowers.

"Why are you proud of me?" she repeated.

"Because you did something I surely couldn't have done—got a raftload of scared people through boiling rapids without a scratch."

"You don't get scratched on a river."

"No, only battered and drowned!" he said. "I got plenty worried. Hell, at some spots I was actually scared, but you never stopped smiling."

"It's my chosen work," she said. Then something ironic occurred to her. "You really ought to be less proud of me now, not more."

When he heard that, his seeking hands halted upon her ribs. She wanted him to slow down, to give her time to think before passion took over.

"What on earth do you mean?"

"Well, you see now, Byrne, how easy it was for me to wade into cold water to find Ronnie. I've sometimes had to jump in after kids who've fallen out of the raft and couldn't make it to safety. I've got a lifesaver's certificate, too."

"You've got a big heart and no egotism," he observed. "I love you, Amy. Let's make love."

"Huh?" That wasn't a question, so she didn't need to answer yes or no. She didn't. The darkness hid her slow smile.

His hands made perfect cups for her breasts, and his heavy breathing warmed her cheek, her throat, and

144

once her sweater was off and gone, he kissed the breasts that he cherished.

"Byrne, Byrne!" With a paroxysm of desire she pulled open his flannel shirt and urged him upon her, pressing her naked back down into the fleece of his coat.

"Could you love me, dearest?"

"I could. I do."

"Oh, honey!" His voice broke. His hands slid under her shoulders and tangled fingers in her hair as he passed his lips fervently over her face. Her lips reached for his, still hungry after so much food, but this food was better, sweeter, more filling. She wanted to be filled, to be one with him, with Byrne, her love.

The moon hung in the sky above the trees like a platinum medallion; Byrne wore its light like a halo around his head. When she stroked his nearly invisible face, he caught her fingertips between his lips and nibbled them.

"Are you cold, my love?"

"No. Quite the opposite," she said.

His big body was a furnace, its heat welcome on this chilly, windy night in the mountains. She wasn't bruised and battered from the rapids and hoped he wasn't hurting much. She didn't want to be careful. She longed for a vigorous, loving wrestling match, no holds barred.

Inside his opened shirt her bosom pressed against him, making both of them sigh in tender remembrance. This was the way they'd come together on the day they'd met, the way they should—if it were possible—forever enjoy the best of love.

145

Tenderly he lay on his side and withdrew her jeans from her legs; Amy cooperated. He undressed as well.

"My brave, beautiful, warm, loving woman," he said, then dipped his tongue tip again into her mouth and into each ear, tantalizing, rehearsing for the final entry for which she ached.

Under the June moon, occasionally catching the scent of smoke drifting downstream from the campfire, Amy and Byrne pledged their love with sweet kisses and tender fondling of the silken cores of their pleasure.

"I want you," she said simply, when her mounting desire threatened to surge out of control.

"I want you, and I love you," he said. "Will you tell me that you love me?"

"I love you."

Now she'd said it. She'd known it months ago, but now she'd said it, making it real for them both.

Byrne moved over her, centered his body above hers, and as she opened to him, he smoothly and expertly filled her. Half his weight was borne by his elbows and knees; he was a considerate man. Under the little tent of his flannel shirt, thrown over him against the chill, they lay on the coat that had helped preserve Amy's life. Moving in unison, they made it last, savoring the pleasure, the incredible intimacy.

Finally, Amy breathed, "Now . . ." and the ground seemed to move like the raft she could still feel in her bones as he thrust harder and deeper. She clutched him to her with all her strength.

"Amy, marry me!" was his cry of culmination.

She saved her breath and her strength to make the ecstasy last. What had he said? Marry him? Already?

She adored him, but weren't they moving too fast through unscouted waters?

## CHAPTER SIXTEEN

Byrne Cooper lay on his back on the damp grass, Amy's head resting in the valley between his shoulder and chest. He'd done it. He'd made love to her and then proposed. Now he awaited her answer.

She was silent, but she wasn't unkind. "Come closer, onto the coat, off the damp ground," she urged, tugging at his body. She began wriggling her legs into her jeans again.

He obeyed. He'd gotten into the habit of obeying this skillful, lovely woman on the trek down the river.

What had a marital expert said on his show years ago? "The reason men hate women bosses is that when they go home at night, they have to doubt their right to dominate their wives."

While his mind meditated on that, his heart was still focused totally on Amy. He kissed every available portion of her sweet body before she again hid it from view; he hindered rather than helped her get dressed, but she didn't seem to mind.

"You're a sweet man," she whispered, kissing him on the mouth.

"Would you resent it if I said that an idea for a talk show just occurred to me, one involving you?" he blurted out. Too late, he realized that his timing was awful. He'd anger her or hurt her feelings.

"You mean a show about Ronnie?"

"No, about role switching. About a man who spends a day taking orders from a woman more skilled than he is and then makes love to her at night."

She mused for a minute. "That's intriguing," she said. "Some guys, I imagine, would lose their ability to perform."

"That's what I was thinking, too. As for me, it only enhances lovemaking that we're equals: you run a raft, I run a talk show. I'm also relieved you aren't upset about talking shop at a time like this. Thanks, Amy."

"Well," she said pensively, "if you'd started rattling on about stocks and bonds, I'd poke your eye out, but you're thinking about us."

"I certainly am!" He embraced her in a bear hug, so full of love that the idea of losing her was like death itself.

"Marry me," he said.

After a pause she asked, "When?" She was trying to be funny, to put him off, to play for time.

"The sooner, the better."

"We'd better get back to camp. We'll wake up everybody, bustling into those tents in the dark."

"We don't have to go bustling into the tents. I took the precaution of putting one sleeping bag outside the men's tent, Amy. It's big enough for two."

"You think so?"

"Yeah. We can pick a spot a little way off, out of sight of camp, and be sure we wake up before the others do."

"That's not a bad idea."

When they got up and finished dressing, he tried to put his fleece-lined coat on her, but she'd settle for no more than sharing it, walking close by his side, under his arm, with his coat draped over both of them. Neither one got cold.

"When am I supposed to go on TV?" she asked him cheerfully, as if she'd forgotten all about his marriage proposal. He didn't like that. If her answer had been no, he'd have a goal to shoot for—changing it into a yes. The way she'd calmly switched the subject made him distinctly uneasy.

"You got any other man in your life, Amy?"

She halted. "Do you think I'd— You think I'd make love to you if I were interested in someone else?"

"I'd hope not, but—"

"It's tough for me to believe that you don't have a bunch of girl friends down in Charlotte, Byrne. I saw how popular you were with the ladies, remember?"

"Don't remind me of that evening," he said, "that blasted dinner-dance. No, I do not have a woman in my life, right now. There's no one but you.

"I'll lay it all on the line, Amy," he continued. "I got engaged twice, once at twenty-one and once at twenty-eight. In each case, one of us realized that a marriage wasn't likely to last. Since we disliked starting out with the notion of divorce as an escape hatch, we split up. Now I know myself better, and I think I know you, Amy. I don't want to grow any older alone. I'm in love with you to stay. Let's legalize it."

He hoped that his cool, analytical style would work better than his involuntary, impassioned cry of "Marry me!" Amy was a sensible woman with her feet

150

on the ground, her paddle in the water. He waited, but she didn't respond to this proposal either.

"What is it, Amy? There's not another man, is there? It's not my age or yours? Look, I love the wilderness. You wouldn't have to give it up for a dull urban life. When I can afford a small plane, we can fly away on weekends. I know of pretty places even closer to Charlotte, state parks, lakes . . . I'm dying to move out of my condo and build a house in the woods. What's the problem? Am I rushing you too fast?"

"You don't even know me very well," she answered. Her voice was soft and doubtful, like a little girl's— Little Red Ridinghood's.

"If I don't, I am ready, willing, and able," he said, "to find out every detail about you."

He felt her body flinch at the phrase "every detail about you."

What was it? Had she been married before and not wanted to tell him? No, she said she'd escaped marrying a potential wife beater. Had she slipped up and borne a child out of wedlock? That didn't bother him one bit. Did her mom's multiple marriages embarrass her? Hell, he didn't care what sort of mother-in-law he got, especially one who lived three thousand miles away in California. Amy was worth a huge sacrifice, and he couldn't imagine anything that could keep him from loving her and eventually making her his wife.

Amy had never enjoyed a more wonderful night. She didn't sleep much, crushed against Byrne Cooper in a sleeping bag made for one, but lying awake, she felt warm, loved, and safe. Even if a black bear out for a stroll accidentally stepped on them, as a bear actu-

151

ally had one time when she wasn't in a tent, she would be able to laugh it off. The bear would be more frightened than Byrne if big Byrne awoke with a roar.

When she roused, she studied how different his sleeping face looked, full on and in profile, at various times as the moon sailed east to west across the sky. One moment he was a sharp-featured Tatar. Then he turned into a slumbering boy. He was her fierce Cherokee captor or Daniel Boone himself.

So he wanted to marry her; he wanted her to marry him.

She wasn't ready to make that kind of decision yet. Why couldn't he rest content with her big decision to go public about saving Ronnie? That was enough to occupy her mind without thinking about marriage, too!

Heck, if he could invent new topics for talk shows while he held her in his arms, so could she. She'd come up with another one: Tradition has it that the chief goal of girls is to catch a husband, while boys rush to escape. However, statistics show that husbands are more content with their marriages than wives are. Reaching their goal makes a lot of women miserable, but failing to escape makes men happy? How about discussing *that?* she thought.

The cure for Amy's depressing morning-after cynicism was close at hand—very close, in fact. She concentrated on Byrne's heavy-lidded eyes until they slowly opened. He awoke. What followed was a perfect distraction. They made love again.

No problem here. If she could spend her time making love with Byrne Cooper on the hard ground under the sighing trees beside the murmuring river, she'd be a happy woman. But what about marriage—a return to the spotlight with a public figure as a spouse?

She'd already volunteered to go back into the spotlight, though. She'd be on TV this coming week, and if she or Byrne didn't display the tabloid photo of her soaked and nearly nude, they'd be stupid. That was the angle they needed to attract a big audience. They'd capture the audience for their message about saving drowned children and adults as well.

After their sweet lovemaking, much quieter and calmer than their happy grappling on the grassy cliff six hours before, Amy dozed off in Byrne's arms. The taste of him was on her lips; the imprint of him, in her flesh. He was her man. Her eyes flew open fifteen minutes later.

Would he still want her if she were different, like an insect metamorphosed into something else? He adored what he thought she was—a nature-loving rafting guide and switchboard operator. She was also a child saver who'd been adopted into his family. When he learned about Evelina Sloan, he'd suddenly see a runaway from Malibu who as a child and teen-ager had been spread over more tabloid pages than he'd ever guess. The woman who he thought had grown up on a farm really sprang from a nest of luxury and license outside Hollywood.

What would Mike and Sheila Cooper say? Byrne admitted that his sister-in-law wouldn't be comfortable at a dinner dance where liquor was served. What if Sheila's new sister, Amy, turned out to be—what would Sheila and Mike call it?—the offspring of a lost soul?

Immediately Amy regretted even thinking in terms

153

like that. Her mother had done the best she could. Yet Amy dreaded facing the Coopers' scorn or, even worse, seeing them try to hide their dread and disapproval. How would they explain to Billy and Ronnie why Aunt Amy wasn't coming around anymore?

She woke up kissing Byrne, cheered by his good humor so she could giggle with him as they adjusted their garments and rolled up the sleeping bag as small as possible. They crept back to the camp like a couple of AWOL soldiers.

"I hope we weren't missed," he whispered, giving her a conspiratorial squeeze.

"Only Irene saw us leave, and she understands."

"She's a broad-minded friend on the French Broad River?"

"Yes," said Amy, shooting him a look, wondering how broad-minded he and his would be about a woman in Beverly Hills whom coarse people referred to as "that sleazy ol' broad Evelina."

At breakfast the sausages tasted as good as they sounded, sizzling over the open fire. The wind was down, and back on the river, people paddled more skillfully today, working out their stiffness. At noon almost everyone stripped to a bathing suit and hopped into the water to drift downstream with the raft. Before they dried out, Amy decided to honor tradition. They mustn't miss anything they'd paid for.

She steered the raft closer to shore and managed to maneuver around behind Irene's raft. Without being obvious, Amy armed her rafters with bailing buckets. Then they sneaked up on Irene's raft and bombarded Irene and her six squealing paddlers with buckets of water.

"Yee-haa!" Byrne yelled, slinging water over their opponents.

Magically everyone started sloughing off the stiff self-consciousness of "maturity." Amy was always astounded to see adults so intensely at play. Her two pudgy grandmothers looked astounded, too, until they were dowsed. That got their ire up, and they dowsed the dowsers in the other raft, working in unison, outdoing all the children on the trip.

Nobody stayed even remotely dry. On that long, quiet stretch without white water, the two rafts bumped together and rebounded. Amy and Irene, doing the steering and most of the paddling, yelled encouragement to the combatants.

They'd all reminisce about this for the rest of their lives.

After the guides had declared the water war over, a beaming Byrne Cooper set to work bailing the raft, which now resembled a kid's wading pool set afloat. Hot sun dried their hair and their shoulders, suntan lotion came out to be passed around and shared. Twelve strangers had become friends.

Rafting did that for people. The more dangerous and frightening the ride, the quicker everyone gave up self-consciousness and reserve and bonded with the others. It might take all day on this more placid river, but up on the Gauley, rafters became comrades after shooting only one Class V or VI rapid. She'd told Byrne about the one called Pure, Screaming Hell, which proved terminal if the guide didn't enter it correctly; the raft simply would not come out at the other end.

"I'm glad you survived that," he'd said in a flatteringly hushed tone of voice. So was she; there'd have been no Byrne Cooper up in West Virginia waiting to treat her for hypothermia.

Amy suddenly had another small revelation. Like rafters bonding after enduring danger together, she'd bonded with all the Coopers the moment she hauled their child from Mackay's Pond.

Bonding—there was yet another good topic for a talk show! She was certainly learning to think just like Byrne Cooper.

## CHAPTER SEVENTEEN

Irene located an out-of-work rafting guide who could sub for Amy, leaving her free to drive back to Charlotte with Byrne. With relish, Irene moved from her apartment in town into Amy's cabin to "furburgersit."

"You couldn't have timed this better," Byrne observed. "I've got several of my TV shows slated, but there's leeway to plug in the show about Ronnie. I want to lead off with it, in fact."

"I may sink your show before it's half launched," she said, only half kidding.

"Not a chance! What I'm wondering is how you'd feel about my featuring the tabloid photo of you. How does that grab you?"

"Well," she said thoughtfully, "you can't throw away an angle like that. I'd do the same thing in your shoes."

"Great!" He reached across the seat and squeezed her hand. "Boy, you don't do things halfway, do you, champ? When you decide on something, you jump in with both feet."

"And with all my clothes on," she said, "which you so deftly removed."

"I sure did." His dark eyes settled on her face and

157

caressed it like a touch. "I love you, Amy, dressed or undressed, wet or dry."

"Stubborn or cooperative," she continued, "bossy or acquiescent, running away from you or courting attention on TV—"

"I love all those things; they're what make you so fascinating, you little chameleon. Compared with you, the average woman is damnably predictable. I never know what you'll decide to do next. Now you'll be my first guest on a TV show that's really mine. I've done call-in TV talk shows, but never in this format, with the host hopping all over the place in front of a live studio audience like Phil Donahue."

"Better a live studio audience than a dead one," Amy retorted, hiding her astonishment. She wouldn't merely be facing cameras? She'd be facing a sea of staring faces, too?

"The audience will act like corpses if I don't invite guests that are interesting enough," he said.

"You'll do fine. Donahue can get me engrossed in the dullest topics imaginable. I can never turn off the TV when he's on."

"I'm not Phil Donahue, Amy, and the thing's moved awfully fast. An established TV personality was all set to host the show, but suddenly he took off for California. They offered it to me, but till now I haven't been able to line up any guests more intriguing than the leads in a counterculture play which is opening in town and three people who'd managed to lose a hundred pounds each on some miracle diet. Those guests are interesting, but they haven't"—he flipped a hand in the air—"they haven't immediacy. What is more gripping than a child who is brought back from the dead?"

"And she's an adorable little blonde," Amy added, "who may be persuaded to chatter away on TV so that nobody will even notice me, pray God. . . ."

"I hope Ronnie goes over big," he said, "but you're even more intriguing. People won't identify with Ronnie. They'll identify with you and ask themselves, 'How would I act in a similar situation? Would I court praise and honor, or would I just slip away?' The fact that you risked your life and then fled, refusing to take credit—"

"But I didn't flee fast enough to avoid being photographed nude," Amy interrupted. "I wouldn't be surprised if some nut accused you of setting up the whole rescue. You got famous for saving me, and then you exulted in print over the sexy mermaid with the wonderful breasts!"

Byrne actually blushed; Amy smiled when she saw this. His blush would have convinced her, had she not been convinced already, how badly he'd been misquoted.

"Not a chance," he said, "I'm sure you don't mean that seriously, Amy. No, if I'd stage-managed your flight and your—your 'exposure,' I would've exploited it immediately, not waited from March till July."

She made a face at his use of the word "exploited." Was she being exploited? Was Ronnie to be exploited?

The national media had certainly exploited Evelina Sloan and her little blond daughter. Grown-up Amy wondered to what purpose reporters had peered into her and her mother's lives in Malibu and printed unfair gossip about them. Why had so many agents and

159

producers urged Evelina's nubile daughter to cut a record, pose for a magazine spread, or try out for a role in some B movie?

The answer was pretty obvious: because there was money in it, not only for Evelina but for them—a whole lot of money.

There were, however, no fast bucks involved in a discussion of resuscitation; that was for sure! Amy's research had taught her that several medical centers were doing research into comas and resuscitation. Maybe they'd get increased funding from more publicity; just maybe. One thing for darn sure: More lives could be saved.

"What're you thinking about, darling?" asked Byrne. "You look so solemn and intent."

"I'm figuring out what I ought to say on TV."

"I know you'll do a super job without any rehearsal."

"The folks at that dinner-dance who were dying to know where on earth you dug me up will get their curiosity satisfied," she remarked.

"Right," he said.

She watched him closely but didn't catch any hint of dread in his voice or on his face. He wouldn't be ashamed, then, of the Amy Barrett he thought he knew so thoroughly?

Sheila, Billy, and Ronnie Sue would fly into Charlotte shortly before the taping in front of a live audience. The show would be aired two evenings later. Byrne figured that Sheila and the kids needed no preparation. It was best that they appear natural and uninstructed.

160

Byrne showed Amy the previous day's newspaper. It announced that Byrne Cooper's first TV show would feature the mystery woman who rescued the miracle child—Byrne's own niece. Amy didn't much like the strong emphasis upon her, but if it would help make Byrne's new show succeed, well, she'd have to grin and brave the exposure.

Prior to taping this spectacle, she and Byrne had lunch with the physician scheduled to be the medical expert. Amy asked a dozen questions stimulated by her reading, causing Dr. Marsch to say, "You've really done your homework, Ms. Barrett."

From Byrne she suddenly received one of the warmest congratulatory smiles she'd ever seen. Amy fell a little further in love with this guy who hadn't a petty, jealous bone in his body. He hadn't received a compliment on his medical knowledge; he was glad the doctor had praised hers.

"Glory be!" as her Carolina-born friends would say. Shouldn't she say yes to Byrne Cooper if he proposed to her once again?

Down at the TV station Amy took a peek through a technician's window into the studio where the show would be taped. The audience, about a hundred people, seated in rows of theater seats, was made up of both sexes, but women predominated. After all, it was midweek and midday. A lot of the people were middle-aged, and many leaned forward with expectation. They knew they were on hand for something new and different in their community.

Amy was allowed to wait offstage, where she could observe Byrne from the wings. After the theme music he strolled out onto the low, oval platform, microphone in hand.

"Welcome," he said, "to the first show in a new series. This station takes the plunge into excitement and controversy. Welcome to the *Byrne Cooper Show.*"

He was graceful, well spoken, and incredibly handsome in his dove-gray suit and blue tie, his river-rafting suntan golden above the crisp white collar. Amy wished they'd retained the radio show name, *Conversations with Cooper.* The less show biz, the better.

Byrne himself had choreographed the show like a dance, proving himself not only a good talker and psychologist but a clever director as well. The hour would not begin with everyone onstage at once—host, doctor, children, rescuer, and mom. He was going to trot them out one at a time for maximum dramatic effect.

To begin with, what did he materialize from out of nowhere and flourish before his rapt audience? There was the tabloid newspaper featuring Amy in bikini briefs and a faceful of wet hair! Amy winced.

"Today, to introduce my new TV show," he said, "I am prepared to turn a travesty into a triumph and a near tragedy involving my own family into a beautiful story of self-sacrificing love."

Unable to see the audience, Amy heard the whole mob, in unison, let out a tender sigh.

Byrne would just love that. As the old saying went, he had them in the palm of his hand. She hoped he wouldn't make a slip and drop them.

"The gallant young woman in this photograph, until today anonymous, saved the life of my brother's little girl," he explained.

"Rhonda Sue Cooper drowned in an icy pond up in

162

Hendersonville last March. Who'd think that anybody underwater for fifteen or twenty minutes would have a chance of survival? Nobody. I didn't have one shred of hope. In fact, I tried to prevent Ronnie's rescue."

The audience made an indignant grunt, as if he'd hit each one of them right in the solar plexus.

"I thought that my niece hadn't a chance in the world. I saw this woman"—he shook the tabloid at the audience—"some unknown woman, fully clothed, wading in the pond at dusk. All of us who rushed there when little Billy raced home to get us begged her to come out of the water. She was endangering her life."

He paused for effect, scanning the audience.

"And then she disappeared under the surface and came up holding our Ronnie Sue. Ronnie was dead—cold, blue, very obviously dead."

No one made a sound. Amy stopped breathing, too.

"If I'd had my way—and I consider myself a well-educated man, informed about first aid—no one would have tried resuscitation on Ronnie. But the rescuer used her last shred of energy to gasp, 'Use CPR; resuscitate her!' Someone did so. Not I; I had no hope. Ronnie's mother was also screaming for resuscitation. Someone humored two foolish women while I wrapped up the woman who had saved Ronnie, trying to get her warm."

He opened the tabloid. "These quotes attributed to me are entirely false—out-and-out lies. I'm displaying this so-called newspaper only to salvage some good from it. You've read it; I'm telling you not to believe it. The truth is what you'll see today. But now we have to break for a word from our sponsors."

163

Amy relaxed. Wow, what a showman! He'd been wasted on radio. His gestures, his indignant scowl, his cadenced delivery as he strode up and down in front of the audience, were spellbinding. Waiting for the commercial to finish, she hardly noticed that off camera he was arguing with someone in the audience. "Lies," she heard Byrne snap. "Why'd you show up here?"

Then Byrne straightened up and got rolling again.

"Enough from me. My niece, who was dead, is now alive. Now, for the first time on television, you will see a modern miracle. I give you Ronnie Sue Cooper."

Sheila, in the opposite wings, gave Ronnie a little push, and the tiny girl had the courage to march straight out onstage to Uncle Byrne, who bent and scooped her up. The audience groaned out a sigh, then began applauding. Ronnie raised small pink hands and applauded right back. Byrne kissed her cheek. Amy heard people sniffling.

Byrne's voice quavered a bit when he said, "This is an occasion for rejoicing. You're witness to a miracle."

The tabloid lay spread open on the floor where he'd dropped it to pick up Ronnie. Not by accident, he stepped right on the page that had the photo of him and the salacious misquotations. He gave it a little kick out of his way.

"Now I want you to meet Ronnie's mother, Sheila Cooper, my sister-in-law," he said. "She had a big role in saving Ronnie's life, too."

Sheila came out; head held high but knees obviously shaking, she had Billy by the hand. The applause redoubled.

"And here is Billy Cooper, who twice ran like crazy

for help. He brought the rescuer to save Ronnie, and then he ran home to get help."

Billy, in either fright or bravado, was swinging his arms like a tin soldier. The bright TV lights dazzled him, and he collided with his mother's leg. The audience laughed affectionately. He waved, then hid his head behind Sheila. From Byrne's arms, Ronnie pointed and said loudly, "What are all those people doin' here?"

Even Amy doubled up in merriment.

Byrne guided Sheila and Billy to chairs on the small stage and clipped microphones on them both. Billy swung his legs and squinted. Still holding both Ronnie and the microphone, Byrne Cooper cleared his throat.

"Now for the big surprise, ladies and gentlemen. As I said, without her brother, Billy, Ronnie wouldn't be alive today. Without her mother, she might be dead. But surely she'd be a corpse in the ground today if a stranger hadn't been driving near Mackay's Pond in Hendersonville on a cold March evening this year."

He turned in Amy's direction and extended his arm. "You've waited long enough to see her, more than three months. Today, in our studio, I want you to meet the mystery woman, the rescuer. Ronnie is a miracle child, and here is the mystery woman, who performed the miracle."

Amy couldn't move. He was waiting for her, arm extended, but she couldn't get under way.

Byrne recognized paralysis when he saw it. He whispered to Ronnie, set her down on her feet, and like a windup toy, she came trotting straight toward Amy. Staring down, Amy saw the little hand reach up

165

for hers. She took it. "Come!" commanded Ronnie. Amy obeyed and appeared onstage.

The applause was a roar, an outpouring of surprise and admiration, excitement and gratitude.

Tears began to wander down Amy's cheeks.

# CHAPTER EIGHTEEN

Amy's first words might not have been wise ones, but they were the only words she could say.

"Here's the person who saved *me,*" she murmured, gesturing toward Byrne.

"Uncle Byrne," said Ronnie, on her way back to her mother. She tried and failed to climb up into Sheila's lap. A woman nine months pregnant does not have much lap. "When are we goin' home?" she whispered —right into Sheila's clip-on mike. Her amplified question brought down the house. Thank heaven for comic relief.

"Amy Barrett," Byrne said, putting his hand on Amy's shoulder, "left the scene of the courageous act because her own hypothermia confused and disoriented her. She also didn't much like being rewarded by being photographed . . . in a state of undress. She was undressed, as you well know, because wet clothes might have chilled her to death."

Amy escaped from center stage to sit down quickly in one of the two empty chairs. Byrne clipped a mike onto the collar of her green blouse. Below her flowered skirt she tucked her bare sandals beneath the chair. How did one sit comfortably and gracefully in front of one visible audience plus an invisible, enormous audience-to-be of television viewers?

Byrne walked up the aisle. "Forgive me for running on so long. We still have one other guest to introduce, a medical expert, but perhaps you have a question for Ronnie's mother or for Amy Barrett first."

Hands shot up. Amy blinked. Already? What on earth would they ask?

"How'd you know she wasn't dead?" a fierce-faced man demanded.

Amy swallowed, leaned forward, and said, "I believed Billy when he said she'd been in the water a short time. A child's head is so small that the brain can cool down before the heart stops beating. A chilled brain can survive on very little oxygen from the blood."

"Why didn't your own brain freeze?" a black woman asked.

"I kept my head out of water except for one moment. Luckily I didn't pass out."

"Mrs. Cooper, is your little girl normal now?"

Sheila explained that Ronnie still had some catching up to do. There were gaps in her memory of events before the drowning. "She doesn't like to get in the bathtub either," said Sheila, causing warmhearted laughter.

Byrne introduced Dr. Marsch, who fielded questions of a technical nature. He named the drugs Ronnie had received and mentioned other young survivors with good prognoses.

The hour flew by, Amy as intent upon admiring Byrne's skill at mediation as on fielding questions from the audience. Ronnie Sue wandered off the stage and captivated the first row by her solemn examination of each person's face.

"You ought to get the word out," one old man stood up and insisted. "My nephew's little kid, she drowned back in the fifties. Somebody might've saved her. There's all sorts of kids out there."

"Remember, Ronnie Sue had an ideal combination of conditions," said Dr. Marsch. "She's small, she was immersed suddenly in cold water, and she was immediately resuscitated." Then he added, "Yet some adults also have survived, and water that's seventy degrees at the surface may be much colder a few feet down."

"You can be pretty sure that Ronnie will be on network TV before long," said Byrne. "Nobody's trying to keep her survival a secret."

In mute astonishment Amy watched a balding man wearing a suit in the front row reach out as Byrne strode by and jerk the microphone out of his hand. He bellowed into his captured mike, "I'm sure everyone will want to know that the mystery woman featured back in March on page one of our nationally distributed newsmagazine is none other than—"

Byrne was about to grab his microphone back, but the man's taunting tone and excited face halted Byrne's hand in midair.

"This young woman, Amy Barrett, conceals the fact that her own mother is the famous singer Evelina Sloan!"

The audience murmured noisily. Byrne whirled toward Amy, and she gave him the smallest of nods. Grabbing his mike from the man, he said, "I don't see any relevance in that!"

"Which shows how little you know about show biz, Mr. Cooper!" he retorted, jeering. "You didn't even know it, did you?"

"No, I did not."

"Even though you and Ms. Barrett are romantically involved?" he shouted over the excited stirrings and mutterings of the audience.

"We aren't—" Byrne corrected himself. "When you wrote those lies back in March, I didn't even know Ms. Barrett. Now she's like a member of my family, and we've become good friends, yes."

Sheila Cooper said nothing. When Amy forced herself to glance over at her, she saw a blanched face. No, there was no longer a chance that Sheila wasn't familiar with the reputation of Evelina Sloan.

As for Byrne, he'd so far avoided characterizing Evelina, even indirectly. Amy could see how hard he was pondering before he could rescue them by introducing another commercial.

During the break Amy sat up straight and announced, "I won't run away from *this* issue. Who my mother is has no relevance whatsoever, Mr. Whoever-You-Are. Why can't you mind your own business?"

"Why do you hide out in the mountains? Why did you run away after performing a heroic deed?" he demanded, not needing a mike. "The people want to know." He stood up, turned, and faced the audience. "Don't all of you want to know?"

Byrne looked capable of throwing a punch.

"It might be none of our business," said an old lady sweetly into the mike that Byrne thrust at her the moment that the commercial ended.

A good thing Mike Cooper had elected to stay home

170

in Hendersonville, thought Amy. She didn't have Mike also to worry about. As shy as his brother was bold, he'd preferred to watch it on television. Maybe he'd miss this fiasco? Fat chance!

"Are you an alcoholic and a pill popper like your mother?" yelled the man from the tabloid.

"Are you all aware that eight thousand people drown each year in the United States," Dr. Marsch put in gamely, "and most of them are children?"

Billy, who obviously wondered what was now going on, got out of his chair, came over to Amy, and asked, "How's Abercrombie?"

"He's just fine," she whispered, longing to pull him up into her lap but afraid of Sheila's reaction. Did the silent Sheila Cooper think she was tainted? Would Sheila snub her or attempt to grin as she bore the burden of knowing Amy's background?

"I think that loudmouth man ought to be thrown out," said one woman, motioning toward the gossipmonger.

"We don't eject people from this show—much as we might be tempted to," Byrne said through clenched teeth.

"Aw, c'mon, Cooper!" the man shouted, still without the benefit of a microphone. "This gal is making your show! You won't generate interest like this again!"

"That's enough," Byrne said so calmly and pleasantly that Amy became really afraid he'd punch out the boor.

"Of course, you could marry your mermaid right on the show and invite your new mom-in-law to sing at the wedding," he suggested.

Mercifully the show had come to a close, and Byrne managed to drown out the man and say good evening to TV viewers who had not yet seen the tape-delayed show.

Amy couldn't believe she was still in her chair, that she'd neither fled nor leaped on that louse to strangle him. She was even able to think about the press coverage that this confrontation would receive. Her mother's notoriety would ensure an enormous audience for Byrne's show the day after tomorrow. Could she expect Byrne to edit the unpleasant interchange out of the tape? Ratings were vital. What a way to begin a new TV series!

As about half the spectators began to file out of the studio, the others clotted at the stage, reaching up to shake Byrne's hand, to gaze at Ronnie and Sheila, Billy and Amy. Bodies insulated Amy from the Coopers, and at this painful moment that was just fine with her. Even finer were the words a young woman was whispering.

"*I* think your mom's a great lady," she confided. "She's had a rough life, but she still hangs in there, belting out the blues."

"Thank you for saying that," Amy murmured.

"Glad to see you turned out good," said an older woman, studying Amy with the searching curiosity that she'd attracted all her life, before she'd gone under cover. Amy had almost forgotten how it felt to be in the public spotlight. Now all these eyes were focused on her like hundreds of flashlight beams. She'd just have to learn to get used to it again.

*I'm grown up now,* she told herself. *I've had eleven*

*years to myself, as a vacation, a strength-building long holiday.*

And now she had her own claim to fame, something she'd done by herself and something she still had to do for other people, people who might otherwise suffer what Dick and Jan Glouster had suffered.

Byrne managed to approach her and lay a hand possessively on her shoulder. "I'm sorry," he said. "I felt like punching the guy out, but that wouldn't have given you more privacy, Amy; it would have meant more press."

She sought in his face what his reaction was going to be. The crowd was thinning out, concentrated mainly around little Ronnie now. Amy couldn't decide what to say next, but that must be progress! She'd never before considered options besides flight and concealment.

Sheila and the children had dropped out of view. Byrne kept an arm around her shoulders as he guided her out of the studio and then out of the TV station into the late-afternoon sunshine. The sun was blinding her even before the two cameras started clicking.

"Dammit to hell!" Byrne barked, putting his body between Amy and the photographers. "Where the hell are you freaks from?"

Why ask? Amy had a good idea where they were from—from the same tabloid as the man inside, for one. The second reporter said politely, "The *Charlotte Observer,* ma'am."

So fame was going to be heaped upon her, starting right now. Okay, *c'est la vie,* let it be. Sighing, Amy suddenly experienced a calmness that allowed her to ease Byrne aside.

"All right," she said to the reporters. "What do you fellows want to know? Let's get all the facts straight this time."

"Amy?" Byrne said, as if he didn't recognize her any more.

Amy murmured into the two microphones pushed close to her face, "If I make use of my mother's fame, it'll be to talk about helping little children."

"Amy," said the more slickly dressed reporter familiarly, "is it true that you and Byrne Cooper are an item?"

Her wonderful new sense of aloof calmness did not desert Amy. "An item?" she asked quietly. "Would you define your terms, please?"

The local reporter shouldered him aside. "When did you last see your mother, Miss Barrett? Have you considered a singing career? What do you *do* up in Hendersonville?"

"I run rafting trips. I have no musical talent."

"Which one was your father?" asked the tabloid reporter. "And was your mother married to him?"

"Joseph Barrett, my father, was my mother's first husband; he is now deceased," she stated without emotion.

"I see."

*How odd,* thought Amy, *the more open I am, the less eagerly he pursues.*

She asked the tabloid reporter, "How would your paper like to print a correction of that article about me back in March?"

"We never print corrections."

"I didn't think so. Well, what more do you want to know?" She advanced a step toward him, and the man

174

actually stepped back. She'd won a retreat, if not a retraction. When she looked up at Byrne, she glimpsed the grin he was trying to disguise.

"Let's go, hon," he said.

"Where are you going?" the duet asked.

Cocking her head confidingly, Amy responded, "Now that's a good question. What's your suggestion? Come on. Why just report—or misreport—the news when you can create it?"

Maybe she'd wake up and remember her words with horror, but right now she was enjoying the opportunity to throw back what the reporters had flung at her. Never in her life had she faced down a reporter, a Hollywood agent, or one of her mother's sleazy hangers-on. Like hunting dogs, they loved to pursue any creature that fled. Today, when she forced herself to stand still, then actually invade the tabloid reporter's own space, he began to back off. The reporter from the *Observer* had good manners; he even sent her a conspiratorial wink.

What an important discovery to make before she got an ulcer or got any older.

"Way to go, Amy," murmured Byrne into her ear.

Yeah, it sure was the way to go and to live. She'd done well. It was all over and done with, all the fleeing and hiding.

"Where're Sheila and the kids?" she asked Byrne.

"I'd better run back in and see."

"Please do."

Both reporters exited. The new, calm Amy Barrett tried to remain calm also about the matter of Sheila Cooper, but her new friend, practically her sister, was still nowhere to be seen.

## CHAPTER NINETEEN

As she saw Byrne disappear into the crowd that had lingered to listen to her interview, Amy wondered for a moment if she wasn't being too sanguine. What did Byrne himself think—really think—of the new Amy Barrett, the daughter of Evelina Sloan? This Amy was newsworthy for sure. Could he separate a woman with a useful "angle" from the woman he'd recently wanted to marry?

A man came out onto the steps of the TV station and invited Amy to be filmed for this evening's local news. Unafraid, she said yes and was gently escorted back through the door.

"Where's Sheila Cooper?" the young TV man asked, "Byrne Cooper's pregnant sister?"

"Sister-in-law," Amy corrected him.

Byrne didn't reappear until Amy's interview was over thirty minutes later and she was heading out of the TV station. He came bounding up the front steps, coat off and tie askew.

"Sorry I had to desert you," he said. "I drove poor Sheila and the kids home to my place. You know where she disappeared to after the show? She made a dash for the ladies' room to throw up."

"Oh, my gosh! The baby's not coming, is it?" Amy's

groan of sympathy was sympathy for herself as well as for Sheila. So the news, the news about who Ronnie's new godmother really was, had nauseated Sheila. *Did she imagine that my mother,* Amy wondered bitterly, *would become, in effect, her little Ronnie's grand-god-mother?*

"Sheila's never spoken in front of an audience before," Byrne hastened to explain. "I gave her an antacid tablet to calm her stomach."

"You really think it was just stage fright?"

"Oh, sure. Remember that poll a few years ago that asked people what would frighten them the most? Was it fire, snakes, blindness, cancer? No, the thing feared most—by far—was speaking before a large audience."

"You'll have to do a show on that topic," Amy said.

"Good idea," he said, not catching her sarcasm. "You did great. You didn't seem a bit nervous on camera. I suppose you faced a lot of cameras as a kid?" he asked, looking at her searchingly.

"Enough," she said. "There were always reporters around."

"I imagine."

His expressionless face and flat tone of voice told her the answer to her unspoken question. She'd lost him, too. She'd lost both Byrne and Sheila, meaning also Mike and Billy and Ronnie, if not Great-grandma Ruby. She was again set adrift, with no family to love and be loved by, and no lover either.

"Where do we go from here?" she forced herself to ask in the same flat tone he'd used.

"In a minute we'll head back to my condo," he said, "to see how Sheila is. A good thing the reporters didn't get hold of her, too. She would've upchucked right on camera."

"Why don't you drive me to a motel or to the bus station?" Amy suggested. "I'll catch a bus home the way I did once before."

"Are you crazy?" he asked her. "What's going on here anyway?"

"What's going on, Byrne, is that I've just had my cover blown. My seamy origins have been exposed; the great deception is over, and your family has varying success at concealing its response. Sheila throws up; you don a mask, but your voice betrays you."

"What're you talking about? Right now I'm headed back to see the film editors, to have them edit out of the tape the remarks of that creep from the tabloid. That was the same jerk who interviewed me after you rescued Ronnie; you'd think they'd have the sense to send someone else. I'm not going to air those insults aimed at you and at your poor mother."

"Poor mother?" she echoed, not believing what she'd heard.

"The mom out in California wearing tights and caftans is actually none other than Evelina Sloan," he said wonderingly, "and you never let on! I remember magazine photos of Evelina and her cute little kid in their matching outfits, and . . . that was actually *you!*"

"That was me," she admitted. Balancing her center of gravity very carefully so her heart wouldn't get jarred, she waited.

"I feel like a fool," he said. "Here we were so very close, but you wouldn't confide in me."

"Win some, lose some," she said, brows arching—still waiting.

"Wait right here. I'll go talk to the film editors."

She let him get halfway down the corridor before she started running.

"No, Byrne! Leave it in, all of it!"

He spun around. "Not on your life."

"I can stand the publicity if your family can. That confrontation makes me newsworthy. It may get me on even bigger talk shows. More people will know about Ronnie."

"You're not kidding, are you?"

"They'd pay my way," she said, "to New York, Chicago, and maybe even to L.A., where I could see Mom. I haven't been out there in ages. I actually like doing television. You can see that I do."

He stood there gazing at her, his shoulders slumped a little as if half the wind had been knocked out of him.

"You do mean it. You're not being cynical or self-sacrificing?"

"I figure, if you've got an angle, use it."

He shook his head. "You're doing this for me, I'll bet, to make sure my first show gets tremendous ratings."

"Maybe I am partly. You saved my life, remember?"

Neither of them spoke for a moment. Then Amy said, "I want to go straight home. You take care of Sheila and call me in Hendersonville when the offers come in for more TV appearances. Think of the stir after I'm in the tabloid again. Please drop me off at the bus station, Byrne."

He gave her a dark look and didn't say a word. He went across the parking lot to his car and unlocked it. She had little choice but to follow him and get in. He didn't drive to the bus station, though; he drove to his condominium, parked, opened her door, and helped her out.

Amy maintained a stony silence.

"I know my sister-in-law," he said grimly as they rode up in the elevator. "Your assumption about Sheila insults her, Amy. We'll deal later with your false conception of me."

In the hall outside his door Byrne halted and bent his head to speak softly. "I'm going to walk in as if I've arrived alone. You stay in the entryway and listen."

"But—"

"No 'buts.' I know Sheila. This is the quickest way to correct your misconceptions, Amy."

She did as she was told. They entered his condo, and he strode through the dim foyer into his living room, while she paused in the shadows. Ronnie and Billy ran to greet him, and Sheila's voice was clearly audible from offstage.

"Byrne! Where is Amy?"

"She'll be coming along pretty soon."

"Oh, Byrne, I feel so awful about this!"

Amy swallowed. Here it came. A woman can judge another woman far better than a brother-in-law can.

"About what, Sheila?" Byrne said loudly, cueing her.

"About Amy's being Evelina Sloan's daughter!"

Amy turned toward the front door, eager to retreat.

"How do you feel about it, Sheila?"

180

Sheila's tone of voice made Amy picture her clasping her hands before her chest, staring up at Byrne.

"No wonder she wanted to avoid publicity!" Sheila said. "No wonder Amy was so vague about herself. And *I* was the one who forced her to go public. I dragged her over to our house to meet the couple who lost their little boy— Oh, Byrne, it just makes me sick!"

Amy, listening intently, postponed for a moment her flight from the condominium.

"Is that why you threw up, Sheila?" Byrne's voice inquired.

"Yes, that plus nerves. Oh, why didn't you stomp on that terrible man before he tried to humiliate Amy? You could have thrown him out! How are we going to apologize, get her to forgive us?"

"Forgive us?" Byrne said.

"Yes, don't you feel guilty, too? She's nothing like Evelina Sloan. Think of the fame and money Amy must've given up to live in that little cabin, working for a pittance! Now that we've shoved her back into the limelight again, she gets ridiculed for having an infamous mother. She doesn't deserve that, Byrne. People are responsible for the kinds of kids they bring up, not for the kinds of parents they got!"

"I know Amy will be gratified to know how you feel," he said. "I think I hear her coming in right now."

Amy hadn't accomplished her escape. She was standing like a statue in the dim foyer when Byrne reappeared, to tug her unceremoniously by the arm into the bright, sunny living room.

The first thing to hit her was Sheila, who practically

leaped across the room to throw both arms around Amy. The unborn baby made it hard for her to reach, but she strained to hug her. The kids bounced up and down in delight, which turned to puzzlement.

"Why are you cryin', Amy?" Ronnie demanded.

"What's wrong?" Billy asked.

"She's had a hard day," Byrne Cooper explained. "She had to go on TV twice, though you were on just once."

Amy didn't want to let go of Sheila, and Sheila held on tight, patting her back as if Amy had been the one who'd almost thrown up on camera.

"I wanted to tell that guy off," Sheila said. "Down at the studio I wanted to jump up and say you'd probably had a rougher life than anyone else there, but look what you turned out to be—a wonderful, loving, brave woman; our lifesaver."

"You got any Life Savers?" Billy asked, eyeing Amy's purse.

Byrne wore the smuggest I-told-you-so look Amy had seen in years, but his gaze was lit with affection as he extricated her from Sheila's grasp.

"Come here, champ," he said, crushing her against him, kissing her till Billy said, "Yuk! That looks silly!"

"It feels great," murmured Byrne. "Amy is great. As for her TV debut, I am very much impressed. As something of an expert in such matters, I can say she's a natural. Cool as a cucumber—"

"Unlike me," Sheila put in.

"You spoke so well, Amy; you came across as strong, controlled, and sensible, with a perfect voice for radio or TV, low-pitched and resonant. That's much rarer in women than in men. Sopranos sound shrill."

"No, I'm *not* going to become a singer, Byrne!" Amy started struggling.

"Hey, I didn't have that in mind at all! What I'm getting at is this, Amy. How about being cohost on my show? That's something to think about—you and I on TV, like the coanchors on the news."

"You're kidding me!"

"No, I'm not, and I'm not exploiting your second-generation fame either. At least I hope I'm not. I'd like to try it whether you had Evelina as a mom or not. I hope we're married by then."

"Married?" she exclaimed, still hardly able to speak or move, standing supported by his encircling arms.

"We could call it *The Byrne and Barrett Show;* how does that sound?"

Amy burst out in laughter through her tears of relief.

"Oh, that's terrific," said Sheila, clapping her hands. "And marriage! Amy, you'd be my sister-in-law and Ronnie's and Dilly's aunt! We'd never lose you then."

"You really do want me in the family? With my antecedents?"

"How can I convince you?" Sheila cried. "You think I'm some sort of crazy bigot? You're what Byrne's been searching for all his life, and you brought my child back to life. I wouldn't mind if you had a Mafia father and a dozen Communist uncles!"

"Wow," said Amy. "I didn't need to keep Mom a secret after all?"

"Frankly," said Sheila, dropping her gaze shyly,

"I'd like to meet your mother. It would be scary, her being so famous and colorful, but—"

Amy reached over and hugged her. "Mom's dried out now, you know. She went to a famous rehabilitation clinic last winter and got off both drugs and alcohol. She's also been married for all of five years this time."

To make Sheila and Byrne as cheerful as she was, Amy said, "Hey, Byrne and I could host a TV comedy show and call it *Grin and Bear It.*"

"Hey, that's a double pun," Byrne said exultantly. " 'Barrett' is also 'Bare It,' as in 'bare your heart to me.' "

"You take a while to catch on, Byrne Cooper!" said Amy fondly.

"Which'll it be, Byrne and Barrett or Barrett and Byrne?" he asked. "That does sound like a striptease followed by an orgy."

Sheila finally recognized their puns. "Brother Byrne," she cried theatrically, her big grin betraying her, "*do* watch your language in front of my innocent little children—three innocent little babies!"

## EPILOGUE

The next time Amy went public, video cameramen came up to Hendersonville to her cabin. Abercrombie and Cornflake thus could have their furry faces televised all over the Southeast, along with Amy's. She held Ronnie on her lap while discussing the rescue with Sheila, who held on her lap the new baby, Amelia Anne. It would be too confusing to have a pair of Amys in the family; when Sheila finally agreed with Amy, she compromised on Amelia.

That homey little film clip was featured on a number of interview and news shows produced on both the East and West coasts. Sheila and all three children accompanied Amy to New York, and yes, to Chicago, too. Sheila's stage fright improved, the kids developed a sort of comedy routine, and Amy stuck in a few plugs for the sort of drug rehabilitation that her mother had recently benefited from.

In Los Angeles her mother appeared on a television talk show right beside her, sitting on the same couch. The film clips shown that day featured not only Ronnie petting Amy's collie but also Evelina and little Amy back in the sixties at a film premiere.

"I want to meet this fiancé of hers," her mother gushed, after belting out a love song that rocked the studio. "I'm so thrilled that my daughter has emerged from the forests and doesn't go around barefoot in a bearskin anymore. No kidding, she's never taken a penny from me, you know. She's the only one of my ex-husbands or offspring who hasn't traded on my fame and come around for a handout."

Evelina gave Amy such a fierce, sudden hug that beads and sequins jangled together. The show's incredibly handsome host grinned.

"When will you take your mom rafting on the river with you, Amy?"

"I'd drown for sure!" Evelina said with a hoot. "Remember, I am, underneath all these face-lifts, a woman almost sixty years old!"

Amy gaped. Mom had never admitted her age in public or in private before.

"And I recommend the clinic," she said. "If my Amy can go around pushing resuscitation, I can push drug and alcohol rehabilitation. We might go onstage as a duo, tapping our way through 'Resus and Rehab! Boop-ah-dee-boop-boop, oh, yeah!' "

Amy broke up in laughter. Drying out hadn't dried up her mother's wild sense of humor. She could just see all the Coopers back in North Carolina staring bug-eyed at their TV screens.

"Can't do it, Mom," Amy said. "I've already signed up to cohost a talk show in Charlotte with the man who'll soon be my husband."

"No joke?" said their host, leaning forward. "What'll it be called?"

*"Controversy with the Coopers,"* she said proudly.

186

Back in Charlotte things moved very fast. Her rafting partner, Irene, was getting married in December, so Amy and Byrne bought out Irene's share in the business. Amy had the notion that poor kids from the city and handicapped kids, too, ought to go rafting on her river, so they put a couple of people to work on that. A house was speedily going up five miles outside Charlotte, in the woods where there was running space for at least two furburgers.

"I want Evelina on our show," Byrne said.

"That'll be no problem at all. When I live in a house with two bathrooms and a patio, Mom will come visit. On our show she'll knock everyone's socks off."

"You knock *my* socks off, Amy," Byrne said. "C'mon, let's go get married."

"Is it the big day at last?" she said teasingly. "Shove off. You're not even supposed to see me on the day of our wedding."

Sheila hurried in from her kitchen, her brow furrowed. "That's right, Amy. It's not traditional for the groom to see the bride. . . ."

"She's not in her gown yet," he told her. "Okay, okay, I'm going, I'm going. See you at the church at eleven."

"Am I pretty?" asked a small voice from the vicinity of Amy's left thigh.

"You are adorable, Ronnie Sue!"

Amy, still in her yellow jump suit, knelt and kissed the little girl, who hadn't been able to wait any longer to put on her pink lace and taffeta dress. She was already carrying her basket of September rose petals, too, holding it very carefully in both hands.

"I thought we'd never see the day," said Mike

187

Cooper, trying to comb Billy's cowlick down. "I hope he doesn't drop the ring."

"It sure won't be a swinging California wedding," Amy mused. "I like your style much better."

Amy stood in the foyer of the little white church overflowing with people and with enormous floral arrangements sent from Beverly Hills. Magnanimously her mother had decided to forgo the wedding so that it wouldn't turn into a three-ring national publicity event.

Amy's gaze ran fondly over the two little towheads —one in lace, one in a sailor suit—who would precede Sheila, the matron of honor, and Irene, the bridesmaid, up the aisle. Grandma Ruby waved from the second row on the right. Three-month-old Amelia Anne burped noisily. Amy slipped her hand through the arm of Byrne Cooper's tall white-haired father.

The music began.

"This is it," she whispered to herself, seeing, near the altar, Mike Cooper in a matching gray tux standing solemnly beside his brother.

Byrne caught her eye and smiled crookedly, blinking hard, all choked up over the woman in white satin who was coming toward him up the aisle.

"My family." Amy's lips formed the word as she passed by so many more Coopers.

"My family, and best of all," she whispered, her face beaming at Byrne, "my dearest beloved."

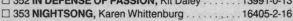

# Candlelight
## Ecstasy Romances™